THE IT GIRL IN ROME

DON'T MISS ANNA'S OTHER ADVENTURES.

THE IT

in Rome

GIRL #3

KATY BIRCHALL

ALADDIN M!X

New York   London   Toronto   Sydney   New Delhi

ALADDIN M!X
Simon & Schuster Children's Publishing Division
1230 Avenue of the Americas, New York, New York 10020
This Aladdin M!X edition January 2019
Text copyright © 2017 by Katy Birchall
Originally published in Great Britain in 2017 by Egmont UK Limited
Cover illustration copyright © 2018 by Jamey Christoph
Also available in an Aladdin hardcover edition.
All rights reserved, including the right of reproduction in whole or in part in any form.
ALADDIN and related logo are registered trademarks of Simon & Schuster, Inc.
ALADDIN M!X and related logo are registered trademarks of Simon & Schuster, Inc.
For information about special discounts for bulk purchases, please contact
Simon & Schuster Special Sales at 1-866-506-1949 or business@simonandschuster.com.
The Simon & Schuster Speakers Bureau can bring authors to your live event. For
more information or to book an event contact the Simon & Schuster
Speakers Bureau at 1-866-248-3049 or visit our website at www.simonspeakers.com.
Cover designed by Laura Lyn DiSiena
Interior designed by Greg Stadnyk
The text of this book was set in Electra.
Manufactured in the United States of America 1118 OFF
2 4 6 8 10 9 7 5 3 1
Library of Congress Control Number 2017954834
ISBN 978-1-4814-6368-3 (hc)
ISBN 978-1-4814-6367-6 (pbk)
ISBN 978-1-4814-6369-0 (eBook)

For anyone who has ever felt
they're not cool enough:
You're wrong.

1.

"YOU CAN'T KEEP ME TRAPPED UP HERE FOREVER!"

Jess folded her arms, looking *very* pleased with herself. "Sure I can."

"Let me down at once!"

"Let me think about that." She acted thoughtful for a moment, stroking her chin, and then shrugged. "No."

I huffed as my best friend looked up at me, a victorious grin on her face.

"You know, Anna," Jess began, "it's not difficult. You tell me *exactly* what happened yesterday and I will put back the ladder so you can get down from the attic. Everyone is a winner."

"I don't see how I'm a winner in this situation," I argued, shining my headlamp around me just in case there happened to be a spare ladder handily up here somewhere. "I'm going to tell Dad to never open the front door for you again. I hope you have thought through the consequences of your actions."

"I have considered them deeply." She smiled, bending down to get her camera out of her bag. "I'm pretty sure this is worth it." She pointed the lens up and I heard a sharp click as I peered down angrily at her.

"Well, that is definitely a keeper." She laughed, examining the image. "You look so angry! Also, you are very pale. Wow, like a ghost peeking out from the darkness of the spooky attic. Good thing we're going on a school trip where you'll see a bit of sun. You could really use some vitamin D."

"You know, you are being extremely insulting."

"I guess the headlamp isn't helping," she continued, completely ignoring me. "With that on you look like a mole. A ghostly mole."

"Seriously. Very rude."

"Actually, maybe more like a ghostly guinea pig. I can't tell. Let me go ask your dad what he thinks. You wait there."

"WHY ARE WE FRIENDS?"

As Jess walked off to consult Dad on which rodent I resembled, I kicked myself for listening to him this morning when he insisted that my big suitcase must be stored away in the attic, and then for thinking it would be a good idea to go and get the stupid suitcase myself instead of asking him to get it for me.

Of course, I couldn't have guessed that while I was rummaging around in said attic, headlamp attached, that my unfunny best friend would come over and steal the ladder, using it as a weapon to gain information because I had refused to tell her some minor details about a date.

Well, I wasn't going to let her win, I decided as I heard Jess's footsteps returning to the landing. I would have to find another way of getting down. There wasn't much in the attic that could help me in this predicament, but I'd have to be resourceful and think outside the box.

"Your dad reckons you look more like a ghostly guinea pig than a mole, but I'm still undecided. How's it going up there?" Jess called as I tried not to sneeze from all the dust I was disturbing in the search for materials to aid my escape.

"What is going on?" I heard my dad ask, attempting to join in on the fun.

"I'm refusing to let Anna down from the attic until she tells me all about her date with Connor yesterday," Jess explained.

"Right," Dad replied as though that was totally a rational thing to do. "You haven't read about it in the papers or online? I can show you if you like. It's just awful."

"THANKS, DAD!" I yelled.

"I don't trust reporters to give the whole story," Jess

informed him. "But I can't imagine it was as bad as they made it out to be."

"Oh," Dad said gravely. "It was."

I groaned. "You're not helping, Dad. Shouldn't you be working on your book?"

"I was actually doing some baking."

"Classic procrastination. And you always have a go at me when I have homework and I . . . *Aha!*" I cried victoriously, coming across some old curtains that Dad had never thrown away.

I shuffled eagerly back to the gaping hole in the floor with my new find and began to lower the curtains down. "I am just like those dudes in *The Great Escape*!"

"Anna"—Dad coughed—"did you just compare yourself getting out of an attic to British soldiers escaping from a German prisoner-of-war camp?"

"I will simply tie this material to something up here and climb down it," I announced proudly to my audience, ignoring Dad. "And, Jess, you thought you were clever! You thought you could defeat me! HA!"

Jess reached out and yanked the curtain hard so that it flew out of my hands and landed in a heap on the floor next to their feet.

"*Oi!*"

"I quite liked these curtains, but your mother forced me to take them down," Dad piped up, nudging them with his toe. "They might come in handy. Thanks for the reminder that they exist, Anna-pops!"

"No offense, Mr. Huntley, but they look like Dog vomited the sixties on them." Jess patted him sympathetically on the arm. "Your taste is terrible."

"Fine!" I switched off my headlamp in defeat. "I'll tell you about the date and you can put the ladder back." I wrinkled my nose. "I think I might be losing air supply."

"I'll leave you girls to it," Dad chuckled, walking back down the stairs. "I look forward to Danny's arrival when I might hear some sense in this house."

"Come on, then." Jess reached for the ladder teasingly. "Fill me in."

"I was dressed as a Teenage Mutant Ninja Turtle."

"Which makes total sense for a first date with the boy you've liked forever."

"Right."

"I was joking. What were you thinking going on a date with Connor dressed as a TURTLE?"

"Because it was the London Comic Con!" I protested as

she shook her head. "I went as Michelangelo. He's the best one. You know, the one who likes all the pizza and says stuff like 'cowabunga!'"

Jess looked at me blankly.

"Really? Nothing?" I sighed and carried on. "So there I was dressed as a turtle and Connor was dressed as a Jedi and at first when I saw him I was kind of disappointed because I wanted us to match and I'm pretty sure that when I said we should go as Teenage Mutant Ninja Turtles he agreed that was a really good idea, but he must have changed his mind at the last minute or maybe the shop had run out of green face paint or something. And then I wished that he had told me he'd made a last-minute decision to go as a Jedi because I could have gone as Princess Leia, although her outfit choices are questionable and I don't think I could have pulled off the hair. I guess I could have gone as R2-D2, though, which would have been quite cute, so he should have told me about changing his mind, don't you think?"

"Oh, totally."

I squinted at Jess, trying to work out whether she was being sarcastic or not. "Anyway, the long and the short of it is that when we got to Comic Con, I tripped over and knocked into the leg of someone dressed in a giant Iron Man suit, who in turn fell into the side of the big Marvel comic-book stand, which then collapsed onto everyone inside it and some of the smaller stands surrounding it. A pretty cool example of the domino effect, really. I mean, if we're looking for positives." I paused. "Can I have the ladder back now?"

"So how did you leave it with Connor?" Jess asked, neglecting my request and looking flabbergasted.

"It was so chaotic, what with me running around apologizing to everyone and helping people up, checking they weren't dead and stuff . . ." I sighed. "I got a bit caught up in explaining everything to the organizers and asking people not to take photos of me, so I'm not really sure what Connor was doing. He was probably helping people out from under the canvas. I kind of abandoned him a little." I buried my face in my hands at the memory of it all. "Eventually, he found me and we waited outside in silence for Dad to pick us up."

"He didn't say anything?"

"Not really. I think we were both still in shock. He sent me a nice message after we dropped him off, though. He said that he had a really great time, that I wasn't to worry about knocking over the Marvel stand, that he thought it was actually very funny and that he was disappointed he might miss out on such dramatic events when I'm in Rome." I rolled my eyes. "He must think I'm such a klutz. I *finally* get a boyfriend and I'm already screwing it all up."

"What did you say?" Jess whipped up her head to look at me. "Why would Connor miss out on events in Rome?"

"He's not going. Didn't I tell you that bit already? He told me yesterday right before I took down Iron Man."

My heart sank a little all over again as I filled Jess in on Connor's plan for summer vacation. A plan that turned out to be the opposite of what I was expecting. "I thought we'd be spending two romantic weeks in Rome together—albeit with everyone else there—but he pulled out of the school trip so that he can work on his second comic book."

"He did *what*? No way!" Jess put her hands on her hips. "That is not cool!"

"It's very dedicated of him," I said sternly, reminding myself not to be so selfish. "I am fully supportive of his decision."

Jess snorted. "Whatever. He couldn't take two weeks out of his comic-book drawing schedule to go on an awesome vacation with his friends and girlfriend?"

"Excuse you, but as a fellow talented artist, *you* should surely be the most understanding when it comes to sacrificing a social calendar for your creations. Photography projects surely come before vacations."

"Wrong, you philistine," she sniffed. "The best work comes from capturing moments of truth, for example photographing friends having the time of their lives on their summer vacation, not shutting yourself in a room away from everyone. Tell Connor he will be missing out on inspiration."

"I will be sure to pass on the message." I rolled my eyes. "Now, can you put the ladder back?"

"Yeah, sure, I just can't believe . . . Hang on." Jess held up her hand and sniffed the air. "What is that?"

"What?"

"I think I can smell—"

"Hey, girls!" Dad called up the stairs. "Brownies fresh out the oven! Any takers?"

Without a moment's hesitation, Jess let go of the ladder and darted down the stairs. "Yes, please! I'm starving!"

"Jess? JESS?" I called desperately, listening out for her footsteps coming back up the stairs. "JESS! I need the ladder! I'm still up here! Is anyone listening?"

I switched on my headlamp and a moth fluttered by.

I hate my life.

2.

IT TURNS OUT THAT, WHEN IT COMES TO PACKING, asking your two best friends to come over and help you is very unproductive.

Especially when the two best friends in question are Jess and Danny.

"What is THIS?" Jess held up one of my T-shirts. "You can't bring this." She threw it away from her dismissively.

My yellow Labrador, Dog, equally as unhelpful with packing, immediately galloped excitedly across the room to fetch it.

"Hey, Anna," Danny said before I had the chance to chastise Jess for causing more mess, "one of your dad's sweaters got mixed up with your stuff."

"That's not one of Dad's," I huffed, snatching the sweater from him and holding it to my chest. "It's mine."

"Oh right." He paused. "It's nice. Very . . . trendy?"

Jess snickered. "This is nice. You can bring this." She plonked a summer dress into my open suitcase lying on the floor.

"You guys are worse than Marianne," I sighed, slumping down onto my bed and encouraging Dog to hop up and join me. "You're all a nightmare."

"Yes, it must be so hard when your dad is marrying a super-famous actress and your future stepsister just happens to be Marianne Montaine, the most famous It Girl in Britain, who is able to give you fashion advice," Jess said, rolling her eyes. "What a tough life you lead."

I narrowed my eyes at her. "I don't remember you getting trapped in an attic for hours."

"It was about ten minutes," she argued. "And that was your own fault for being so uncooperative."

"It's lucky you arrived when you did, Danny. A few more minutes and I might have passed out from inhaling too much dust."

He laughed and came to sit next to me on the bed, leaving Jess flinging around clothes from the pile spilling out of my wardrobe, and allowing me to rest my head on his shoulder. "Is that the one about Helena?" he asked, pointing at the glossy magazine sitting on my bedside table.

"Yeah."

I passed it to him so he could admire the picture of my future stepmother wearing a sparkling green sequin dress, her hands on her hips, the wind machine blowing her glossy hair out and an easy-going smile framing her pearly white teeth. "It's weird to think that she's on the front cover of magazines," Danny said, "a famous movie star with a legion of fans . . . and then at the same time she's just Helena, the lady your dad is getting married to. Big year for you."

Um, just slightly. A big year for most people would be, I don't know, passing all your exams with flying colors, for example, winning an academic school prize, maybe, or riding an elephant on vacation, perhaps.

So far this year, this is what has happened to me:

1. I set someone on fire.
2. My dad went to interview a famous actress, fell in love with her, and then got engaged to her. Without my permission, I might add.
3. I started getting photographed for websites and newspapers all the time.
4. They said I was an It Girl, because my soon-to-be stepsister was an It Girl and we became

really good friends, even though she gets compared to Audrey Hepburn in the press and I get compared to ghostly moles and guinea pigs by my friends.

5. I got stuck in a waterfall. Upside down.

6. I got stuck in a plant pot. Bottom first.

7. I got a boyfriend. Which is hard to believe when considering the above.

8. I went on a date with my FIRST EVER BOYFRIEND! Then I destroyed the venue.

"You're missing something," Jess said when I mentioned all this in order to demonstrate Danny's amazing power of understatement.

"I know"—Danny clicked his fingers—"singing terribly in front of the whole school and no one clapping and it was really awkward."

"No, that's not it," Jess said thoughtfully.

"Hitting Connor when he tried to kiss her?"

"That's the one!"

As I buried my face in a cushion, Danny put the magazine down and picked up the Italy guidebook my dad had given me, flicking to the Rome chapter.

"What exactly is there to do in Rome?" Jess asked, making a disgusted face at one of my skirts and throwing it back into my wardrobe. I held on to Dog's collar so he couldn't make a running leap after it. "It's basically all about the food, right? Spaghetti Bolognese and ice cream and stuff."

Danny threw an irritated look at Jess. "Rome is one of the most beautiful cities in the world," he muttered, scratching behind Dog's ears. Dog looked up at him adoringly, his tongue lolling out in appreciation. "It is full of history and culture as well as spaghetti Bolognese."

"Whatever. I just hope a gorgeous Italian guy asks me out. Maybe we can go on a double date, Anna," she said, winking at me.

"I can't. Connor isn't going to Rome, remember?"

"Oh yeah." Jess smiled mischievously. "I forgot. He can't have fun because he's an *artist*." She threw two pairs of flip-flops into my suitcase. "When I meet my dream Italian boy, I'll just have to go on a double date with Stephanie and Danny, then."

Danny immediately went bright red at the mention of his new girlfriend, Stephanie, the girl who I mistakenly thought Connor fancied last semester because she is really cool and artistic and has one of those blunt haircuts that I sometimes find myself staring at because it is just so neat.

"I'm not going on a double date," Danny stated firmly, returning his focus to the guidebook. "I wonder if we'll have time to visit all these recommendations."

"Why wouldn't you go on a double date? Don't you loooooooove Stephanie?" Jess pouted and made kissing sounds.

"Shut up." Danny blushed, throwing one of my pillows at her and making her laugh.

She stood up and rushed over, poking Danny's cheeks and saying, "Are you embarrassed, Danny-wanny-woo-woo?"

"Gerroff!" he yelled as she continued to squish his cheeks. Dog got excited at the commotion and felt left out so he head-butted me.

"OW, DOG!" I cried, rubbing my forehead. "You gave me no warning!"

"Anna! What is all this racket?" My door swung open and Dad stood in the doorway, his arms crossed, his hair sticking up all over the place, his eyebrows leaping around his face at every pronounced syllable. He looked at the state of my room in despair. "There are clothes *everywhere*."

"Hey, Mr. Huntley, you know what would really help our packing?" Jess looked at him innocently. "More brownies. The ones you made this morning were truly remarkable."

"Oh. Well, thank you, Jess," Dad said, his hard expression softening. "Baking is one of my hidden talents."

I snorted. Dad's face immediately switched back to his Anna-I-don't-have-time-for-this-nonsense expression. "Anna, I don't have time for this nonsense. I'm trying to write a chapter about parachutes in my study. It's not easy when you're—"

"I promise we'll be really quiet now," I interjected before he could use this opportunity as an excuse to drone on about how writing another boring book about weapons used in the war is for my benefit because who else is putting bread on the table and blah, blah, blah. I mean, why can't he write interesting books like romantic comedies? Why does he have to write bestselling books on *old* stuff? Probably because he is old.

"How is the book going?" Danny asked politely, as though he were actually interested.

"It's . . . er, coming along, thank you," Dad said, hesitating. "A lot of pressure with the wedding on top of it all. It would be a bit easier if we weren't hounded by reporters the whole time, of course, but"—he smiled—"you have to make sacrifices when you're marrying the woman of your dreams."

"Ew, Dad. GROSS!" I wrinkled my nose.

He laughed. "Right, keep the noise down. I better get back to my parachutes."

"Are you seriously writing a whole chapter about parachutes? What can you even say? They are just big floaty bits of material." Jess shrugged, receiving a pointed look from Danny, which she failed to notice. "I don't think you should write a parachute chapter. If you ask me, Mr. H, I would stick to explosions and stuff. Give the people what they want. Throw in a love story and you're golden."

"Thank you, Jessica," Dad replied drily. "I can't tell you how much I appreciate your advice on my life's work."

Jess smirked.

"Your dad is seriously cool," Danny announced, looking at me enviously when he had gone. "He is writing army books AND dating a movie star."

"All right, Danny, careful you don't drool too much on the pillow," Jess snorted. "It is quite sweet the way he talks about

Helena, though. You can tell they're the real deal even though they're celebrities."

"What does that mean?" I asked.

"You know." She shrugged and picked up the magazine, flicking to a page inside and pointing at the showbiz news pages. "There's always drama with famous people and their relationships. They fall in love, they split up, they start dating someone half their age, they go into politics, they get back together and so on and so forth." She slapped the magazine back on the table again. "Maybe it's because your dad and Helena are older and wiser. It's very refreshing that they're different."

"Your dad is very patient to put up with all the press attention," Danny added solemnly.

"I guess it is tiring for him, especially when he's trying to plan a wedding and write a book. And then I make things worse by destroying comic-book conventions, and the photos are on every front page in the country." I felt my cheeks go hot as I remembered the look on Connor's face when someone insensitively asked him to take a photo of them with me when we were desperately trying to find the exit. At least he laughed about it afterward. "Connor is *very* patient too. He can have a break from it while I'm away."

"Don't worry, Anna," Jess said, moving back to my pile of clothes and beginning to sift through them again. "Look at *Notting Hill.* It worked out for Hugh Grant and Julia Roberts."

"Is Connor really not coming on the trip?" Danny looked disappointed. "Who am I going to hang out with when you girls are being . . . girls?"

"Who am *I* going to hang out with when you're all on your double date?" I said glumly.

Jess rolled her eyes dramatically. "Maybe it's time to make new friends in Rome."

"No way." I groaned as Jess threw one of my skirts across the room. "It's taken me fourteen years to make friends in England. And I speak the same language here. In Italy they wouldn't even know what I was saying."

"That could work to your advantage," Danny said under his breath with a smile before I threw him an evil glare.

"Stop being so pathetic—you are a particularly awesome friend and . . . Hey, Anna . . ." Jess hesitated. "What's this? Wait a moment. Is this . . . is this . . . a CAPE?"

She yanked out a large red piece of material from the pile of clothes and held it up so that Danny could get a good look.

"Does that big glittery gold A on it stand for Anna?"

Danny asked, sitting upright and looking mesmerized by it.

"Uh . . ." I blushed. "No?"

There was a moment's pause before they both burst into hysterical, uncontrollable, tear-inducing laughter.

Note to self: It's time to make new friends in Rome.

THINGS YOU WOULD NORMALLY EXPECT TO HAPPEN
at a bridesmaid dress fitting:

> 1. You are cheerily greeted by the bride and anyone else present.
> 2. You try on your bridesmaid dress.
> 3. The bride and other bridesmaids tell you how wonderful you look.
> 4. You all laugh and discuss the wedding.
> 5. Everything goes perfectly.

Things that happen at a bridesmaid dress fitting when the bride is Helena Montaine:

> 1. You enter the bride's house and are greeted by an angry Chihuahua.

2. You are introduced to the prime minister's wife, who has dropped by for a cup of tea, while an angry Chihuahua slides along the floor behind you, refusing to let go of your shoelace.

3. The angry Chihuahua is removed from your shoelace by a member of the bride's wedding team, and Fenella, the wedding planner, makes a remark when she sees you about how hairbrushes must have gone out of fashion with teenagers.

4. As you wait for the bride's daughter to arrive, your own mother decides to fill the time with demonstrations to the bride and the prime minister's wife of some Chinese martial-arts moves she learned on a recent business trip.

5. Everything is a disaster. And nothing has started yet.

"Sorry I'm late, everyone!" Marianne sang as she breezed into the hall, placing her huge designer handbag down on the ground and whipping off her sunglasses, looking every inch the perfect British It Girl as she swept her glossy brown hair away from her face. "Did I miss anything?"

"Tai chi," I informed her as she came over to give me a hug. "And the prime minister's wife. She just left."

"Sounds like a normal day in Mom's household." She gripped my shoulders. "How are you? After the events of your first date, I mean."

"Trying to forget about it. The Internet won't let me."

"Oh, have I been there." Marianne grinned. "It will go away. Tom thinks you looked adorable, by the way, in that avocado costume."

"I was a turtle, but please thank Tom on my behalf."

Marianne laughed and went over to say hi to Helena and my mom. Tom Kyzer was her rock-star boyfriend, who she was completely in love with, to the point where she could hardly talk about anything else. As a couple they were a particularly big attraction for the paparazzi—they couldn't do anything without the whole world knowing about it. But unlike my dad—and even Marianne, who was indifferent to it all—Tom seemed to love the attention. "I was born for the cameras," he once said to me with a wink.

"So, Rebecca," Marianne said to my mom as she ignored Fenella's Chihuahua yapping at her from the arms of the dismayed-looking man holding him, "I hear that, unlike

Anna and me, you've had the privilege of already seeing the bridesmaid dresses."

My mom smiled mysteriously. "You can never know what it's going to look like until you see it on."

"Speaking of which, let's get going, shall we?" Fenella encouraged our two mothers to take their place on the sofa and bustled Marianne and me behind separate screens that had been set up in the sitting room. Two elegant ladies followed me and began to help me undress.

I heard my mom chuckling about something with Helena on the sofa. Mom is a travel journalist and is often on the other side of the world on some kind of weird assignment, but she was staying in England for the summer. Even though my parents weren't together romantically—they never really had been in the first place—they were best friends, and Mom completely ADORES Helena. So, when it came to the wedding, Mom was very much involved with the plans, and Helena seemed to need her approval on every aspect of it.

"I can't wait to see you girls!" Helena crowed as one of the elegant ladies yanked my hair into a bun to get it out the way, and the other one began to unzip a suspiciously large clothing bag hanging up on the screen.

Marianne and I had already been subjected to a traumatic

dress moment when Helena made us try on bridesmaid dresses that looked as if they had been snaffled from the cast of *Sesame Street*, but I had full faith that everyone had learned from that experience and that Helena's excellent taste as an international fashion and acting icon would shine through.

Hmm . . . whatever was being pulled over my head by various assistants did feel quite heavy.

And there was a lot of puffing going on.

"There we are," one of the ladies said, panting as though she'd just finished a workout.

"You look like you belong in a fairy tale," the other lady whispered as she looked me up and down wistfully.

Yeah, for sure, I did look like I belonged in a fairy tale.

AS ONE OF THE GOBLINS!

"Helena!" I yelped as the lady fiddling with the waistline of the dress practically knocked the breath out of me.

"Divine, isn't it!" Helena exclaimed. "Diana designed them—she's with you right now—so you have her to thank for it!"

The lady who had just finished winding me tilted her head to the side and then smiled. "It's perfect. You look like a princess."

Okay, so I know I'm no fashion designer, but is this

woman BLIND?! She had put me in some kind of lavender monstrosity that contained enough netting to catch a pod of killer whales.

"Let me see!" Helena squealed, and Mom added, "Yes, we're *dying* to see."

Diana shooed me out from behind the screen and at the same time Marianne appeared from behind hers. The expression on her face reflected exactly how I felt.

"Oh, girls," Helena whispered, her eyes welling up.

THANK GOD. She must have realized that this was the worst decision she'd ever made and now it was going to be an absolute pain to change the bridesmaid dresses again—and with hardly any time to go before the Big Day. Plus it would cost a fortune so Dad wouldn't be too happy about it. I actually felt a little sorry for her.

I prepared myself to say in my most comforting and reassuring voice, *Don't worry, Helena, we can achieve this feat together*, when her face broke into a Cheshire Cat smile.

"You look so beautiful! It's just what I wanted—the dresses are perfect!" She jumped up and tottered over to Diana, embracing her, and as a tear of joy slid down her cheek, she turned to us again and said, "I could not be happier. This was so terribly important to me. I'm so proud of my girls!"

I stood in shock, confused about whether there had been some kind of chemical leak nearby and everyone in the room was losing their vision or something.

I turned to my mom for confirmation but even she was nodding slowly, a hand on her heart as she took us both in. I made a face at her, attempting to convey through the medium of my eyes that she needed to speak up and say how awful we looked.

"I think they look splendid, Helena; you are truly talented, Diana. What are you doing with your face, Anna? You look like you're trying to impersonate Fenella's dear little Chihuahua."

"Mom," Marianne began, picking her words carefully, "I love the color bu—"

"Oh, Marianne," Helena interrupted, breezing across the room and pulling Marianne into her arms, which in these dresses—with the skirt poofing out so much—was not easy. She had to go in from a side angle just to reach her. "I knew you'd love it! I am so lucky to have such a wonderful daughter!"

Marianne froze, unsure what to do as Helena dabbed her eyes. They all turned to look at me for my verdict. Marianne furrowed her brow in concentration at me and I knew she was trying to do what I had been attempting with Mom. She was desperate for me to tell the truth.

But how could I? Helena was so happy and the designer was standing next to me and do you know what she was holding? PINS. A load of very sharp pins. I had no choice.

"I think these dresses are just . . . great."

Marianne looked at the ceiling in despair.

"Oh, Anna," Helena cried, coming over to embrace me and stroke the sleeves of the dress lovingly. "Don't you just love all these ruffles?"

"I . . . er, sure do."

"And the skirts are so big and voluminous—I just love them!"

"Yeah." I smiled weakly, trying to sound enthusiastic. "Are you sure we'll all fit down the aisle? Haha."

"I think I need to take it in at the chest," Diana was saying, examining me closely. "I didn't realize you were quite so small there."

Brilliant, thanks for that, Diana.

"Yes, she hasn't developed in that area quite yet."

Wonderful, thank you, Mom.

"If only you could wear this dress to the family dinner we're having before you head off to Rome on your adventure,"

Helena sighed. "Because then Connor could see you in it! Such a shame!"

"Uh-huh. That's really . . . uh . . . That is a big shame."

"We should get out of them now," Marianne said hurriedly. "Don't want to crease them. You know. Any more than they are. Haha."

"Good point, Marianne, you're so thoughtful." Helena clapped her hands. "But don't worry, darlings, just a few more weeks and the whole world will see you in these magnificent designs! Doesn't that just make you want to *cry*?"

Marianne and I exchanged a grimace. Helena had hit the nail on the head.

4.

From: jess.delby@zingmail.co.uk
To: anna_huntley@zingmail.co.uk
Subject: So
Are you feeling nervous?
J x

PS Why aren't you answering your phone?

From: anna_huntley@zingmail.co.uk
To: jess.delby@zingmail.co.uk
Subject: Re: So
Why would I be feeling nervous?
Love, me xxx

PS Dog gave my phone to Hamish. You
know, the Pomeranian that lives down the

road. His owner only just returned
it to me.

From: jess.delby@zingmail.co.uk
To: anna_huntley@zingmail.co.uk
Subject: Re: So
Because you're about to go for dinner with
your whole family. And Connor.
What is it with your dog stealing your
phone?!
J x

From: anna_huntley@zingmail.co.uk
To: jess.delby@zingmail.co.uk
Subject: Re: So
What's the big deal about going for dinner
with my family and Connor?
I think it's kind of sweet what Dog did. Maybe
it was Hamish's birthday or something. Dog is
very thoughtful that way.

From: jess.delby@zingmail.co.uk
To: anna_huntley@zingmail.co.uk

Subject: Re: So

Anna. For the last time. Dog is a DOG. He doesn't understand birthday occasions. He doesn't go out of his way to bring a present to the Pomeranian down the road. He is simply a canine thief.

Anyway, I'm glad you're not nervous or anything. I was just worried you would be because of the time Danny and I went for dinner with your whole family.

You know, when we were at that Turkish restaurant and your mom and Helena joined in with the belly dancers and your dad drank all that raki or whatever it's called and then told us the story about when a director told him he could be the next Brad Pitt, but he turned it down for the, and I quote, "bewitching nature of the written word."

But that's good you're not worried! I'm sure it will be great.

Right. I'm going to shut down my computer now and go check I've got everything ready to go for Rome for the hundredth time.

I'M SO EXCITED!
Message me after. Now that you have your
phone back there's no excuse.
J x

Hi! You've reached Jess. Leave me a message and I'll give you a buzz.

    BEEP

    "Jess. It's me. Anna. You're right. I can't believe I didn't stop to consider the family of weirdos I was born into and the disaster zone into which Connor is about to step. You have to HELP. How do I cancel the dinner?! ANSWER YOUR PHONE."

Hi! You've reached Jess. Leave me a message and I'll give you a buzz.

    BEEP

    "Jess, pick up, this is an emergency. Oh, Lord, I just remembered when Mom and Marianne had just met and Mom told her a story about how she befriended a bushpig in Malawi. WHAT IF SHE TELLS CONNOR THE STORY ABOUT BEFRIENDING A BUSHPIG?! Would you date someone whose mother told you a story about befriending a bushpig? Exactly. It's all over."

Hi! You've reached Jess. Leave me a message and I'll give you a buzz.

BEEP

"Plan A has failed. Dad didn't buy the story I told him about there being a panther on the loose, escaped from London Zoo, and that we should all stay inside for our own safety. Turns out London Zoo doesn't even HAVE panthers. I'll have to come up with a Plan B. What kind of zoo doesn't have panthers? Stupid zoo."

Hi! You've reached Jess. Leave me a message and I'll give you a buzz.

BEEP

"Plan B failed. And now my arms are covered in ketchup for no good reason. Dad is yelling at me to clean up otherwise we're going to be late. Well, the dinner is going ahead. Connor has no idea what he's getting himself into. I'll call you later when I no longer have a boyfriend and my life is over."

Hello! It's Anna here. Leave a message. Okay, bye!

BEEP

"Just got all your messages. What on EARTH was Plan B?"

* * *

"Anna"—my mom chuckled over her salmon—"I think when people ask what you're most looking forward to on a trip to beautiful *Roma*, you shouldn't lead with 'getting away from all the stupid London pigeons.'"

"They're getting out of control. It's like they're plotting, the way they strut around the place," I argued, letting Marianne steal a chip from my plate. "When there's a pigeon on the throne, don't say I didn't warn you."

"They are truly a threat to national security." Connor nodded, throwing me a disarming smile. "Thank goodness Helena knows the prime minister personally."

"Well, yes. You know, he has a wicked sense of humor, although you wouldn't have guessed it from the ties he wears. Anyway, I think it's just fabulous that you get to go on such a trip," Helena enthused. "You'll come back for the wedding completely refreshed."

"And such a place! Ah, *Roma*," Mom sighed.

"What happened in *Roma*?" Marianne asked eagerly as Mom got this dazed look on her face.

"Oh, you know." She picked up her glass, swirled its contents and slowly leaned back in her chair as though she were Gandalf about to tell the hobbits of her great adventure. "I met Alberto there."

"Mom," I groaned, looking at her pleadingly. "Please don't say anything too weird."

"He was a handsome poet and he played a ukulele," she sighed, causing Marianne to giggle and me to put my head in my hands. "I became his muse."

"Oh, Rebecca, how wonderful!" Helena swooned.

Connor and my dad shared a glance and looked distinctly awkward. I slid further down in my chair and became very focused on my glass of water.

"Such a shame that you can't go, Connor," Mom said, tilting her head sympathetically. "It really is a *very* romantic city. You and Anna could have shared some moments under the stars and—"

I choked on the ice in my drink and began to splutter. Marianne knocked me on the back.

"Thanks," I wheezed before turning to give Mom a pointed look. "Anyway, enough about Rome. Let's talk about Connor's comic book."

"So you're going to be working on it for the *whole* summer?" Marianne asked.

"Looks like it." He nodded enthusiastically. "It's sad to miss out on stuff like Rome, but I have to get on with it. And"—he turned to smile at me—"I can spend time with Anna when she gets back."

"I'm sure she'll have plenty of adventures to tell you about!" Helena said. "Plenty of fun and getting into trouble!"

"No, no," I replied in my most sophisticated and grown-up voice. "I will be following all the rules and lying low, drawing no attention to myself whatsoever. The itinerary looks fascinating."

"Ow!" I looked accusingly at Marianne, who had for some reason just kicked me in the ankle.

Helena raised her eyebrows in surprise. "Well, I hope you're not intending on following *all* the rules."

"Actually, Helena, I think Anna should absolutely do so," Dad said sternly, prompting Mom to snort and Helena to shake her head at him in disappointment.

"Well, if you're going to insist on following rules," Helena said authoritatively, rolling up the sleeves of her kimono, "let them at least be good ones."

Helena Montaine's top five rules for making the most of a new city:

1. Don't be afraid to say "yes" to new things, such as local delicacies and traditions.
"I don't think I'd have had half as much fun on

that film set in Dubai if I'd said no to riding that ridiculous creature, the camel. At first I didn't have the slightest interest, but I very much bonded with Ibil in the end. When he stopped spitting, of course."

2. Speak to the locals.

"This is an absolute necessity when visiting a new place because they will be able to point you in the direction of the cleanest lavatory facilities in the area. Indispensable knowledge."

3. Make sure that you visit at least one historic landmark early on in the trip so you can get a photo of yourself next to it.

"Then if you just happen to wander into a luxurious spa and end up staying there for a few days, no one can accuse you of missing out on the terribly important culture of wherever you are because you have photographic evidence."

4. Be sure to learn at least one essential phrase that you will be using often in the local language of where you are vacationing.

"For Italy I recommend attenzione con la mia

casella di cappello, *which means 'careful with my hat box.'"*

5. Make your own rules.

"It is YOUR vacation and you are making YOUR memories. Make sure they are good ones. And by that I mean fun ones."

I laughed nervously as I think I caught Connor frowning slightly at that last one.

"Helena's right," my mom insisted. "This is Anna's first big adventure. She should make the most of it."

"Speaking of adventures," Marianne began, "I actually have my own adventure to tell you about. I'm moving." She beamed. "Tom and I have decided to move in together."

I sat in shock. Marianne hadn't mentioned anything about this to me—I didn't even realize they'd talked about things like that. Judging by the expression on Helena's face, she hadn't mentioned it to her mother either.

"I know it's quite fast, but we're totally committed and we've talked it through extensively. We're both really excited and now seems like a good time. He'll be on tour for the next couple of months so I'm going to be looking for the perfect place and then when he gets back we'll move in."

"Well." Mom smiled, taking charge as Helena looked completely shocked. "Congratulations, Marianne, that's very exciting."

"Yes," Helena agreed, pulling herself together. "It does all seem quite fast but then I'm one to talk. You have to do what makes you happy." She turned to Dad, who smiled back at her in a goofy way, reaching over to link his fingers with hers before kissing her hand.

I mean, I know it's cute that they're so in love and blah, blah, blah, but do they need to do this kind of thing in front of ME?

I couldn't even look at Connor at this point. But he reached over and gave my hand a reassuring squeeze. I blushed and looked at my feet.

"Tom makes me happy. The happiest ever," Marianne gushed, her cheeks flushing pink.

"Well then"—Helena raised her glass—"how exciting. Congratulations, Marianne."

"My goodness, what a summer!" My mom laughed. "Here's to the wedding, Connor's comic book, Marianne's new place, and Anna's Roman adventure!"

As everyone stretched over to clink glasses, Marianne leaned gently toward me so that our shoulders were touching.

"And," she whispered in my ear, "here's to making your own rules."

5.

THE WHOLE OF THE NEXT MORNING I TRIED TO ACT like it was just a normal day in front of Dog. He sat next to me while I brushed my teeth as he always did, and I could see him eyeing me suspiciously as I put my toothbrush in a travel bag and not into its normal mug. Then I saw him look mildly puzzled as I went around the house picking up everyday items such as my phone charger and my shampoo and taking them upstairs to my room, then shutting the door.

"Anna!" my dad yelled up the stairs. "You're going to be late! Rebecca, Helena, and Marianne will be here any minute. We've got to get everything packed up and ready!"

"What's Dog doing?" I shouted back through my door.

"What?"

"I said, what is Dog doing?" I carefully opened my door so I could peer out through the crack.

"I don't know, Anna," Dad said, exasperated. "I think he's

chewing on the Monopoly board in the sitting room. I've told you not to leave board games within his reach. Don't you remember the incident with Chutes and Ladders?"

"So, he's distracted?"

"Yes. He's not passed Go yet." Dad laughed VERY loudly at his own joke.

"Dad, I'm being serious! I need to know the coast is clear for me to bring my suitcase down."

"For goodness' sake, Anna, just bring it down. Do you want me to come and help you with it?"

"No! No, stay downstairs. If you come up here, he might know something is up. Act as normal as possible. Grab some paper and moan about deadlines or say something boring about the war like normal." I heard Dad mumble something about ungrateful teenagers as I opened my door wide enough for me to squeeze through with my suitcase. "Is the front door open?"

"Yes."

"Is the trunk open?"

"Yes!"

"Okay, well, make sure you leave my pathway clear. I'm going to run down with the suitcase and quickly out the door, before throwing it in the trunk without Dog seeing a thing.

If Dog approaches, you need to alert me and I'll run back up and hide the suitcase."

"Alert you?"

"Yes. Secret code. Do a squawk or something."

"A *squawk*? Anna, what are you talking about?"

I sighed at how slow he was being when we were already pressed for time. "That's code for 'Dog is on the move.'"

"Or I could just say, Dog is on the move. You know, because he's a dog and he doesn't understand human speak?" Dad huffed.

"Yeah, that's what you think. I know better. Is the coast clear? Maybe I should hunt out my walkie-talkies. They might be helpful."

"Anna, just come down the stairs and put your suitcase in the car before I lose my temper."

"FINE. But if Dog sees the suitcase and goes crazy because he knows that I'm leaving him, you can't blame ME for anything that gets broken when he punishes me."

"Anna—"

I quietly tiptoed out of my room with my suitcase in tow and began a very slow, careful descent down the stairs with Dad standing at the bottom watching me, his arms crossed. The suitcase was much heavier than I was expecting even though I'd already had to cut down half of what I wanted to bring due to weight restrictions. I could barely lift it up from the floor, so I kind of slid down each step with my back against the wall, straining every muscle so that the case didn't touch the ground and make a noise.

"What on earth are you doing? Why are you walking down the stairs like a crab?"

"I am walking down the stairs *stealthily*," I hissed back. "Keep your voice down. The slightest out-of-place noise will send Dog investigating and then he will see me with the suitcase and go into a FRENZY. Honestly, Dad, you are so unsubtle. You could never be a spy."

But just then my arms failed me and the suitcase dropped from my hands, landing with a loud *thunk* on the stairs and then clonking down every last step before landing at Dad's feet.

Dad and I froze.

We waited for the sound of Dog barging out of the sitting room. No footsteps came and I breathed a sigh of relief and motioned for Dad to quickly pick up the case and take it out through the door. I helped him get it into the trunk, ignoring his grumbling about how I must have packed the kitchen sink and, for goodness' sake, did I really need enough outfits to last me a year? In his day you would go for weeks with just a shirt on your back.

I didn't think it was the right moment to remind him that things had moved on since Biblical times.

As we both turned back to the house, I gasped and stopped still. Dog was sitting on the front step watching us.

We were busted.

He must have seen the whole thing. "Dog," I began in my most soothing voice, "it's not what it seems. I'm just going away for two weeks, but I'm not leaving you and I'll be right back in no time. Dad's going to make sure he gives you extra snacks every day to make up for the inconvenience." Dad snorted next to me so I punched him on the arm. "Now, why don't we just go back inside, sit down, and talk this through like adults."

I saw Dog's eye twitch.

In a flash he was up on his paws, springing back into the house and flying up the stairs at full pelt. "NO, DOG, COME BACK!" I yelled, bolting after him into the house and seeing the tip of his tail sailing into my bedroom. I rushed up the stairs and skidded to a halt in the doorway. Dog was standing on my bed facing me and in his mouth he was holding my phone.

"Dog," I said slowly and calmly. "Let's not do anything rash. We don't want to do something we regret, do we?"

His tail swished slowly from side to side.

"Give me my phone, Dog," I said gently, taking a step forward. He took a step back and shook his head in warning. Dad joined me in the doorway and let out a loud sigh when he saw us both in the position of a highly charged standoff. "Dad, this is your fault."

"*My fault?*"

"I told you that we'd been watching too many John Wayne movies. It was bound to rub off on him."

"Enough of this nonsense," Dad said, nudging me aside and striding forward confidently toward our Labrador. "Dog, drop!"

Knowing he had the upper hand, Dog waited until my dad was close enough and then he leaped down from the bed, dodging him and zooming past me back downstairs. Dad and I chased after him into the kitchen, stumbling to a sudden stop as we saw Dog dangling my phone over his water bowl from his drooly jaws.

"Hellooooo!" Helena cheerily sauntered into the house with Marianne and Mom in tow. "Anyone in?"

They came into the kitchen and saw Dad and me both

standing like statues, watching Dog. "Oh dear." Mom bit her lip. "Did he see the suitcase?"

"Don't encourage Anna, Rebecca. The two things aren't linked."

"Of course they are, Nicholas." Mom sighed. "It's so like you to dismiss something so obvious."

"Dog, it's just two weeks." I knelt down on my hands and knees to attempt a different approach, hoping he might back down if I wasn't towering over him. "I promise I'm coming back. I'm just going to Rome."

On the word "Rome" there was a big splash as Dog released my phone from his jaw and it plopped perfectly into the middle of his water bowl. I closed my eyes in horror and Dog trotted past me with his head held high to go sulk in the sitting room. Soon enough I heard him chewing away on the Monopoly board just to hammer home how he felt about this situation.

"Oh, Anna, your phone!" Mom cried, quickly rescuing it and grabbing a towel, desperately trying to dab it dry.

"You need to put it in a pack of rice," Marianne instructed, going immediately to the cupboards to find one.

"That dog," Dad sighed as I clambered to my feet.

"Don't blame Dog," I said huffily. "It's my fault for not

being honest with him. Anyway, it's about time I got a new phone—that one you got me is ancient."

"Let's discuss it in the car." Dad threw up his hands in exasperation. "Now, everybody in."

I let them all pile into the car and Dad stood tapping his foot, impatiently waiting to lock up as I sat cross-legged next to Dog, who was even sulkier now that Dad had taken away the Monopoly board and put absolutely anything of value out of his reach. All he had to distract him from his sorrows was a gross old tennis ball. I gave him a big cuddle and I think he must have forgiven me because he gave me a lick and a loving headbutt.

As soon as we had come through the airport doors and turned the corner to the check-in desk, we were hit by a barrage of shouting and paparazzi camera flashes.

At first I was shocked that they could possibly know which desk to wait for us at, but then I saw that our teacher, Mrs. Ginnwell, was standing there holding a big sign that said WOODFIELD CHECK-IN POINT.

Helena, a paparazzi professional, immediately took it in her stride, guiding me toward Mrs. Ginnwell and smiling angelically at the cameras as she swanned past in her wide-brimmed sun hat and billowing summer dress. Marianne clacked along in her heels next to her mom, wearing sunglasses that dwarfed her face, tiny denim shorts, and a crisp white shirt, her arms and hands dripping in jewelry. I wish I could look so effortless in front of the national press but, you know, doing something as casual as checking in your luggage becomes much more difficult when you've got a hundred flashbulbs going off in your face and people shouting questions at you.

"Anna, who are you wearing?" (*Actually, funny story—this T-shirt was originally a dress but Dog ate half of it to punish me when I turned the TV off halfway through* Homeward Bound.) "Helena, any wedding dilemmas?" (*Yes, excellent question. Big dilemma, in fact: She is dressing her daughter and her step-daughter up as giant purple hippos.*) "Marianne, is it true that you and Tom Kyzer are on the rocks?" (*Well, you obviously don't have the whole moving-in-together scoop*). "Anna, are you worried about causing chaos abroad after your recent disaster at the London Comic Con event?"

I froze.

The reporter clearly smelled fear: "Anna, do you consider the embarrassment you might cause your friends and family when these incidents occur or do you like the attention? How is your boyfriend coping with the pressure . . . ?" He paused for dramatic effect. "At HOME?"

All cameras suddenly pointed away from the rest of my family and focused entirely on me.

"I . . . I . . ."

Suddenly Dad's arm was around my shoulders, leading me away from the check-in desk and toward the security line for departures. "Here's your passport," he said, placing it in my hand. "What have I told you about the paparazzi? Ignore them."

"But they were asking about Connor!" I felt horrible thinking about how Connor would react to being dragged into the latest news story when he wasn't even here this time.

"They're trying to push your buttons—you know that. Don't let them." He gave my shoulder a comforting squeeze as I nodded.

When we got to the line, the press still swarming around us taking photos, Helena produced a thin box from her oversized handbag that she was now holding out for me.

"A parting gift," she said, smiling. "Just a little something."

"Thanks, Helena!" I took it from her nervously as a hush descended on our audience and rippling whispers of,

"What's in the box?" and "Make sure you get the shot!"

I undid the ribbon, aware of several lenses focusing on my hands and wishing I had practiced an I-love-this-gift expression. I opened the box and peered at the contents. "Wow! Great! Is it a fan? That's . . . handy."

"Let me," said Helena, and, with a dramatic flourish, she lifted the fan and sharply released it, a cloud of glitter bursting from it into the air and raining down on us.

The crowd gasped and then burst into applause as Helena bowed her head to the flashbulbs in acknowledgement, fanning herself elegantly with my gift and showing me exactly how it's done. Marianne may have been wearing her sunglasses but I could *feel* her rolling her eyes behind them.

"What a wonderful present!" my mom said excitedly. "Very useful for the heat in Rome and it's so beautiful."

"Handmade by a charming geisha in Japan," Helena informed her, pointing at the colorful, detailed pattern. "I was filming for a few weeks out there once."

"Thanks, Helena," I said, brushing the glitter off my sleeves.

"I've got you a little something too," Mom said, holding out a bag. I reached for it tentatively. Mom has always had a rather odd taste in gifts because they are mostly relics from far corners of the earth, which isn't surprising considering she's a well-known travel journalist, but my standard response of "Great, Mom, this is so unique" was wearing thin.

I put my hand cautiously inside the bag, ignoring Dad's eyebrows, which were wriggling away in warning, and pulled out what can only be described as a grubby, jagged bit of rock.

"Er—great, Mom, this is so unique!"

"It is for guidance, wisdom, and luck," she said knowingly. "Particularly useful now that you won't have your phone on you to contact us when you need to. But *at least* you have this stone."

I nodded. "Brilliant," I said, and shoved it in my pocket. "That's great. Right, well, I better be going through, then. Thanks for the . . . uh . . . fan and the rock."

I hugged them all good-bye and gave a final wave before joining the line to get through security. Glancing back at my family, who were waving enthusiastically, the press still buzzing around them, I tried to ignore the whispers and pointed looks too, acting as though I didn't know the person behind me in the line was taking photos of my back.

"See you for the wedding!" Marianne cried over the crowd.

"And *try* not to get into any trouble!" Dad added.

I handed over my boarding pass, turning the corner and out of sight from them all, the sudden quiet making my worries seem all that bit louder in my head. This was Connor's time to work on his comic and my time to have a sophisticated Italian experience. Without any embarrassing press stories. Either way, I just had to make sure I didn't get into any trouble in Rome. Easy, right?

I put my hand in my pocket and pulled out the bit of rock. "I hope you work," I said under my breath to it, hoping no one was paying attention to me talking to a stone. I had a feeling I was going to need all the luck I could get.

6.

I SPOTTED JESS CHOKING NEXT TO THE PERFUME stand.

"What's going on?" I asked as she coughed and spluttered all over the place.

"I . . . sprayed . . . the . . . perfume . . . in . . . my . . . mouth."

"No, Jess, perfume doesn't go there," I said, offering her the bottle of water I'd just bought. "It goes on your wrists."

She gratefully glugged the water and then put her hands on her hips. "No kidding. The nozzle was facing the wrong way when I sprayed it. How come it took you so long to get here? Danny, Stephanie, and I have already been around all the shops."

"My family gave me presents before I went through security."

"Going-away presents? That's so cute. What did they get you?"

"A fan and a rock. Where are the others?"

Jess looked confused for a moment by the going-away offerings but didn't comment. She was very used to my weird family by now. "Everyone's in the bookstore. We've got to meet Mrs. Ginnwell in ten minutes by the information point before going to the gate. I volunteered to wait here for you. So, were you okay with all that?" she added, jerking her head back toward security.

"Oh yeah," I sighed. "I set off the alarm about ten times coming through the scanner and they couldn't work out what it was. I thought maybe it was the rock, but they used that handheld beepy thing and it kept going off on my right arm."

I held my arm out to illustrate my story. "But I'm not wearing any jewelry so the security woman was weirded out by the whole thing and that got me thinking: Maybe I'm actually a product of a scientific experiment that went wrong and when I was little they injected me with an experimental serum just like Captain America, but it didn't work out so my parents have kept it secret from me all this time and the only way I've discovered the truth is because whatever chemical runs through my veins sets off airport security scanners!"

Jess lifted an eyebrow. "Yeah, I actually meant were you

okay with all the press out there, but thanks for that really long spiel of crazy."

"Oh." I checked my wrists suspiciously anyway. "Yeah, it was fine. Let's go to the information point."

As we walked, I filled Jess in on the family dinner.

"Marianne and Tom are moving in together?" She looked surprised. "I thought he was on tour at the moment."

"He is. When he gets back, they'll sort it out."

"Ah. More importantly, though, how did you leave things with Connor? Did he give you a passionate good-bye kiss?" she teased, nudging me with her elbow as I swatted her away.

"No! Well, you know."

I felt my cheeks growing hot. It hadn't exactly been the most romantic setting, what with my whole family in the car behind us as we stood at his doorstep.

"Well, thanks for inviting me tonight," he'd said, as I spotted everyone in the car looking very obviously the other way. Except Dad who was having his head forcibly turned by Helena.

"Thank you for coming," I replied. "I hope my family wasn't too overwhelming. They can be."

He laughed. "They were great." He paused, pushing his bangs back. "I'm going to miss you, Spidey."

I blushed at the nickname he'd given me on discovering that we were both big Marvel geeks.

I opened my mouth to say something along the lines of how I wished so badly he could come with me to Rome and was there any chance he could forget about the comic book for just two weeks. But I stopped myself, swallowing my words. It wasn't fair. I should be proud of having such an intelligent and motivated boyfriend who was willing to give up his summer vacations to work on something he was passionate about.

"I'll miss you, too."

"By the sounds of things, I'm not sure you will," Connor joked, looking slightly uncomfortable.

"What are you talking about?" I said, taken aback.

"Oh, you know." He jerked his head toward the car before looking down at his feet. "What Helena said . . . You'll be having too much fun."

"I'd have way more fun with you there."

Connor smiled and reached across for my hand.

"HOOOOOONK!"

I jumped around at the embarrassingly loud car horn just in time to see Helena giving my dad a reproving whack across the head.

Oh my God. Just let me curl up and die in a hole in Outer Mongolia right now.

"Haha. I guess we should be used to having an audience by now." Connor laughed nervously. "At least they don't have cameras."

"Yeah, well, I'm not sure a car horn is much better," I muttered, glaring at my dad.

"It will be nice for you to escape the press in Italy. Plus"—he smiled—"I'll be shut away in my room most of the time working on *The Amazing It Girl* so they can't use me as an excuse to hound you. I'll be away from it all."

"Sure," I said, trying to match his enthusiasm. "Although, you know, it would have been better to get away from it all together."

"I know. It would have." He nodded. "But we'll speak and message all the time, though."

The car honked again and my dad gestured for me to hurry up, pointing at his watch. I felt a little better when I saw Helena give him yet another thwack over the head.

"I better go!" I sighed. "Good luck with the comic."

And then that had been that.

"That's *it*?" Jess looked unimpressed.

"What were you expecting?" I laughed. "A pledge of his undying love?"

"That would have been nice," she said before getting overexcited at all the headphones on display in the electronics store. She ran over to try them all on and I followed, picking up the first pair and shoving them over my ears, immediately shutting out all the busy airport noise with a tragically slow romantic ballad about heartbreak. Not quite what I needed right now, but I wasn't going to show that in front of Jess.

I sighed. The truth was that I was a *little* disappointed at my good-bye with Connor. I don't think some signs of a little more pain and heartbreak at having me leave the country for two weeks would have gone amiss. A *little* tear? The exchange of romantic tokens, perhaps? Obviously nothing gross like in the olden days when they exchanged lockets of hair, which, you know, probably would have creeped me out, but *something*.

I comforted myself with the reminder that Connor was shy and I wasn't exactly the smoothest of operators. And that my dad seemed to have lost control of his senses when it came to what's appropriate in a seeing-your-daughter's-boyfriend-safely-to-the-door situation.

And they say that distance makes the heart grow

fonder. Just like Arwen and Aragorn in *The Lord of the Rings* for example. Or Spider-Man and Mary Jane Watson . . . Anyway, he *had* definitely said we'd speak every day. I'd probably even have an e-mail from him waiting for me as soon as I landed telling me how much he regretted not being able to have a proper good-bye. . . .

Suddenly my headphones were yanked off my head. "Hey!" I spun around to find Jess was standing right next to me.

"Didn't you hear me say your name like a hundred times? It's time to go join the group," she said, placing the headphones back on their stand. "You were in some sort of weird daydream."

"No, I wasn't," I said, feeling my cheeks going hot and picking up my bag.

"Oh, really?" She raised her eyebrows and put my headphone to her ear. "I can't *imagine* what you were thinking about."

We came around the corner and saw Mrs. Ginnwell waiting for everyone by the information point. She was now holding up a large yellow sign that said WOODFIELD ASSEMBLING POINT and was waving a Union Jack with her other hand.

"May I commend you, Mrs. Ginnwell, on your variety of signs," Jess said, as we approached her.

"Thank you, Miss Delby," she replied, gesturing for us to wait by her side. "Any more of that cheek and you'll be making notes on the architecture of the hotel while everyone else is at the end-of-trip party. Understand?"

Jess scowled and I pursed my lips, trying not to laugh. I had to give it to Mrs. Ginnwell, she was taking her job very seriously, making sure the students were all under control. Unlike the other two members of staff, Miss Lawler and Mr. Crowne, who were having a heated debate in the bookstore over the best crime writers, and Mr. Kenton, who I spotted in the arcade playing a zombie game with James Tyndale.

I laughed when I saw James throw up his arms in victory after destroying the zombies, forcing a grumpy-looking Mr. Kenton to declare him the winner and earning a congratulatory high five from his best friend, Brendan Dakers. James has a competitive streak, which admittedly had been very handy when he was on my team last semester for Sports Day, but also, it turns out, can be really quite tiring when he regularly shows up at your door over summer vacation expecting you to join him for a "casual jog."

Clearly I tried to refuse every time because (a) Sports Day was over and we had won so there was no point in doing physical exercise anymore and (b) I'm not an insane person who runs for fun.

But he forced me to go running with him and then kept yelling stupid stuff at me that was meant to be motivating, like "Keep those knees up," and "Winners don't take breaks" and "Anna, try not to fall in the pond this time."

So it really didn't come as any surprise that he would be taking zombie games *very* seriously indeed.

James caught my eye and shot me a triumphant grin. I was giving him one back when Jess elbowed me in the ribs, gleefully drawing my attention to the whining voice nearby coming from the Queen Bee of our school, Sophie Parker. This time she was pompously demanding to know from Mrs. Ginnwell where she could make a formal complaint about the airport.

Danny wandered over with Stephanie. "What's all the fuss about this time?" he whispered, keen not to put himself in the way of Sophie Parker's latest angry tirade.

It didn't work. She fixed him with a death stare. "They took my water at security."

"Just buy a new drink," Jess snorted.

"It wasn't just any drink," Sophie hissed, flicking her hair back dramatically behind her shoulders. Sophie was not Jess's biggest fan. She wasn't particularly fond of either of us, but at least she wasn't threatened by me. In her eyes, I was just one big loser who kept getting in her way. Jess, on the other hand, being beautiful and sporty, was Sophie's biggest nightmare.

"It was an incredibly expensive, special type of flavored water that regenerates your skin cells from the inside out," parroted Josie Graham, sounding like a really bad TV commercial. Sophie's minion, Josie, was never far from her Queen Bee's side and hated me more than anyone else in the school. Probably because I once set her on fire and then another time hit her in the face with a discus. They were both accidents, but it is really bad luck that she should be the victim on both occasions. She looked down her nose at me. "The water is imported—from *Italy*."

"That's the stupidest thing I've ever heard," Jess laughed, causing Sophie to puff up angrily. "Where do you think we're going today?"

"Thank you, girls—that's enough," Miss Ginnwell interjected, before a full-on brawl could ensue. "Sophie, you know you can't bring liquids through security. It's your own fault for not checking the rules. Right, I think everyone is here." Mrs. Ginnwell put her sign down and clapped her hands together. Looking furious about being so easily dismissed, Sophie folded her arms and shot daggers at a smug-looking Jess. "You will all have an allocated seat on your ticket," Mrs. Ginnwell continued. "That is where you will sit on the plane. I don't want anyone swapping or complaining. Is that clear? It will just cause a lot of fuss and make things much more difficult for the members of staff to keep track of you all."

There was an immediate burst of chatter as everyone rummaged around for their ticket and conferred with their friends.

"We're miles away!" I exclaimed, as Jess and I compared.

"We're two rows away, Anna." She smiled. "I'm sure you can cope."

"Hey, I'm in the row in front of you," James pointed out, looking over my shoulder.

"Cool! We can pass messages!" I exclaimed without thinking, causing Jess to cover up a laugh by pretending to have a coughing fit.

"Can we paint each other's nails too?" James grinned.

Swallow me up now, please, ground.

But if I thought that situation was awkward, it was nothing compared to the plummeting in my stomach when I boarded the plane and saw just who I was sitting next to.

7.

"REALLY?" SOPHIE SNEERED AS I SHUFFLED INTO the seat next to her.

"Hey, how is your summer going?" I asked in what was clearly an overly chirpy voice, but hoping slightly desperately that maybe a plane journey could be what was needed to break the frostiness that was radiating off Sophie in waves.

Of course that was fairly unlikely taking into account that since starting at Woodfield I had accidentally and temporarily stolen her boyfriend and then last semester I had beaten her team in Sports Day, something she cared about A LOT, so chances were slim that she would be willing to start afresh.

"Don't talk to me the rest of the flight," she stated, pulling out a silk eye mask from her designer handbag. "And if you fall asleep don't even think about snoring." With that she placed her eye mask on, adjusted her pink neck cushion, and turned away.

I wished Connor had been there. He was very good at ignoring Sophie and knowing exactly the right thing to say to make me feel less of a loser. I wiggled my head around to see if Jess could come over and rescue me. But in the process I somehow managed to knock Sophie's special cushion from behind her neck.

She made a noise that sounded suspiciously like a growl. I yelped and jumped away, then sat rigidly next to her, too terrified to move.

After takeoff, a note flicked through the gap in the seats in front of me and landed on my lap. It was from James.

Dare you to draw on her face. How good are you at moustaches?

I snorted, and Sophie shuffled slightly, shutting me up instantly. I waited until she was perfectly still before quietly ripping a page out of my notebook and scribbling something back.

Want to switch places and show me how it's done? She actually likes you, so the punishment would probably be way less harsh.

67

Chicken.

Pretty rich coming from the guy who is scared of worms.

Anyone would be scared of worms when they are THROWN at their face out of the blue.

Yeah, well, maybe you shouldn't yell at people when they are taking a five-second break from a grueling run.

You had been lying on the grass for twenty minutes. I did several laps of the park while you had a nap.

I didn't have a nap. I spent the time digging up worms to throw at you.

Hey, guess what?

What?

I just peeked around. Jess is fast asleep.

I considered the risks of any movement near Sophie carefully.

I'll get my pen.

We were all so excited about touching down in Rome that not even Josie or Sophie complained when we were piled into the stuffy hired coach after collecting our bags. We stared out of the windows, gaping at the beautiful monuments and buildings as we drove to our hotel, while fashionably dressed people on scooters zipped past us, ducking into narrow, cobbled streets.

I was too distracted to inform Jess that she now had felt-tip cat whiskers on her face.

We burst into the hotel chattering excitedly to one another and it took a while before Mrs. Ginnwell could get us to quiet down so she could be heard.

"You're all in rooms of twos and threes," she said before taking a deep breath, clearly ready for some protest at whatever she was going to say next. "We have assigned the person or people you will be sharing with. . . ." Everyone started groaning. "AND I DON'T WANT TO HEAR ANY COMPLAINING!"

"Please say I'm sharing with you or someone who actually likes me!" I whined to Jess, glancing at Sophie and her minions glaring at everyone else from the other side of the room.

"Don't worry," Jess said, pulling out a hand mirror from her bag to try and brush away the hair that had fallen into her face. "It will be better than on the plane—no one is that unlucky. Lightning never strikes in the same place twi—WHAT IS THAT ON MY FACE?"

"Anna is quite the artist." James laughed, winking at me as everyone looked our way.

"OH, REALLY," Jess began, turning on me.

"Anna Huntley?" Mrs. Ginnwell called out, consulting her clipboard. "You will be sharing with . . . Sophie Parker."

She shook the keys at me cheerfully. I looked at Sophie, whose jaw had dropped to the ground. I turned to Jess. "What was that about lightning striking twice?"

"Well," Jess said, snapping her mirror shut and smiling broadly so the whiskers stretched prominently across her face. "Some people might call that karma."

8.

From: rebecca.blythe@bounce-mail.co.uk
To: anna_huntley@zingmail.co.uk
Subject: Greetings from England!

Hello, my darling girl!

I hope you are having a wonderful first evening in beautiful Roma! Thank you for your phone call earlier. I'm thrilled you arrived there safe and sound. And just ignore your father complaining in the background about the phone bill you were running up by calling on the hotel landline. It's not your fault that Dog broke your phone!

I'm only pleased that Helena and I happened to be at your house when you rang. Your father would have just answered the phone, confirmed you were alive and then hung up.

71

Honestly! I blame the amount of spy books he reads. It closes him off to emotion.

It sounds like quite a cool place if it has computers! You should have seen the places I've stayed at on my European travels.

When I was in France considering a career as a horse whisperer, I was living in what I am now sure was a converted zoo. Hay everywhere.

I think you were trying to tell me something but I couldn't make it out as your voice was too muffled. Were you talking while holding a scarf over your head?

It sounded along the lines of "I'm tearing apart a broom with an oaf" or "I'm swearing at noon with goats."

I may have heard you wrong, Anna, but I do not condone you tearing apart anything, let alone hotel property. In Madrid I once broke off the nose ring of a bull's head that was on the wall of the hotel suite I was staying in and it didn't go down well at all.

I'm also not keen on you stealing goats,

Anna. Unless they need liberating from some evil shepherd oppressor? That would be a different matter, of course. Now that I think about it, I don't remember seeing anything about goats on your itinerary. . . .

Have a lovely time, darling! We already miss you, especially your father. I caught him looking forlornly at your room earlier and he tried to brush it off by saying, "Why can't she leave her room in an acceptable state?" and then busied himself with some fishing flies, but I know it was all a facade.

Ciao!

Mom xxx

From: anna_huntley@zingmail.co.uk
To: rebecca.blythe@bounce-mail.co.uk
Subject: Re: Greetings from England!

I AM SHARING A ROOM WITH SOPHIE.

That's what I said, Mom! I am sharing a room with Sophie!

Why would I be stealing goats?? Why would I be tearing up brooms?? Why did you break

off a bull's nose ring?? When did you consider
being a HORSE WHISPERER as a career?!
WHY CAN'T MY FAMILY BE NORMAL?!
Love, me xxx

"This place is disgusting."

Sophie threw her bags down on one of the beds and strutted over to the window to lift the blinds. "There isn't even a view! It's just some stupid courtyard."

"It's not so bad," I offered timidly, practically grazing my fingers as I ran them along the coarse bed cover. "And courtyards can be cool."

"Courtyards can be cool?" Sophie snorted. "Can you hear yourself when you talk?"

Sophie and I had both desperately tried to protest against the room arrangement, especially when Josie and Jess got assigned to a room together and caused a similar amount of fuss. "It's so easy, Mrs. Ginnwell," Jess argued. "Just switch us around so that Anna and I are together and Josie and Sophie are together."

"For the first time in history I actually agree with Jess Delby." Sophie looked slightly disgusted at this realization before turning sweetly to Mrs. Ginnwell. "I don't see what the problem with that solution could possibly be."

"Exactly." Jess nodded. "Everyone is happy if we just swap and then we don't have to share with people we . . . uh . . . don't see eye to eye with."

"Girls, I'm very disappointed in all of you. For one thing, I specifically said that you were not to complain, and for another thing, it is exceptionally rude to complain so loudly in front of the people you are sharing with."

"Trust me, the feeling is mutual," Sophie said, swishing her hair back.

"Girls, in life you don't always get to pick your team players, but that doesn't mean you are not a team."

"I would NEVER pick these two as my team players," Sophie scoffed, looking Jess and me up and down as Josie snickered behind her.

"I would NEVER want to be on your team considering the last time you captained you lost. Or have you already tried to blank out Sports Day?" Jess smiled triumphantly as Sophie turned bright red, glaring at her.

"That's enough! Really!" Mrs. Ginnwell rapped on her clipboard for our attention. "My decision is final. Anna, you are sharing with Sophie; Jess, you are sharing with Josie. I don't want to hear a peep out of any of you about it, and if there is any trouble, then you will be on a plane back to

England before you can say 'spaghetti.' Is that clear?"

We reluctantly nodded.

"Good. View it as a chance to get to know one another. You're all such *lovely* girls. Sometimes you don't realize just how much you have in common with someone until you're stuck in a room with them."

Sophie grimaced and then turned on her heel, flouncing off toward the stairs with Josie trotting along behind her. Jess shrugged at me as we acknowledged defeat, turning to follow them.

Despite the fact that the very first thing Sophie did on reaching our room was start complaining again—first about the view and then about the lack of complimentary items that were available to us—I found myself optimistically wondering whether there might be any hope of getting along during this vacation. There was a time—when my dad first decided to ruin my life by getting spontaneously engaged to a famous actress and the world suddenly had access to my daily humiliation via newspapers, gossip magazines, and websites—when Sophie and I had been close to being friends.

Sure, it turns out that it was probably only because of the whole It Girl thing, but I was certain there were some genuine moments, especially when she once told Josie off for taunting me. Maybe, underneath the vain, cruel exterior, there was a glimmer of kindness in Sophie Parker.

She noticed me studying her as I thought about a future where we might be civil to each other. "You know, when you stare like that you look like one of those red-eyed frogs that alligators eat."

Aha! Communication—now this was a start. "I'm impressed with your frog knowledge. Do you watch David Attenborough? Was that on a recent episode?"

She ignored me.

"Really," I continued, blazing on with no idea where I was going with what I was saying, "I didn't know that you were into that kind of thing—you know, wildlife and stuff. I watched a David Attenborough episode recently about insects. It was really interesting, actually. Did you know that a bombardier beetle gets back at his enemies by shooting boiling liquid at them? Seriously, they have rotating nozzles in their . . ." I faltered, sensing this might not be the right way to build bridges. "Well, in their *butts*. And the butt nozzles fire out the boiling liquid. Cool, right?!"

Sophie slowly lowered the dress she was holding and put it back in her suitcase. "Oh my God. You are so *weird*." She slid along the wall toward the bathroom, trying to get as much physical distance as possible between us and locked herself in.

There was a knock on our bedroom door. "Anna?"

I opened it to find Jess standing there, scrubbing her face with a washcloth. "I've come here to let you know that I have decided to forgive you about the whole whiskers thing," she declared, walking past me and slumping on my bed. "I thought it best to tell you in person."

"Really, that's the reason you've come here?"

She smiled at me mischievously, still trying to rub the ink off her face. "Duh. It was extremely difficult to tear myself away from Josie. We were getting along so *splendidly*."

"That bad, huh?"

"She has already given me a lecture on how I wear my hair incorrectly." Jess raised her eyes to the ceiling. "How can I wear my hair wrong? It's hair! It's on my head! I had to get out of there. I saw her checking out my fingernails and I was afraid I'd get told I was wearing my cuticles wrong. Where's Queen Supreme, then?"

"In the bathroom. I think I freaked her out by talking about liquid firing out of beetles' butts."

"Yeah, that would probably do it."

"I was trying to make an effort to be friends."

"Sure, and when in doubt talk about beetles and their excrement."

"It's not excrement, it's a boiling-hot liquid that they fire at their enemies."

"Why were you trying to make an effort to be friends with *her*?" Jess snorted.

"I thought there might be something in what Mrs. Ginnwell said. You know, trying to make amends."

"Trust me"—Jess shook her head—"better to let things be."

Suddenly the bathroom door swung open and Sophie peeked around from it wearing her towel. "What are *you* doing in here? I hope this isn't going to be a regular occurrence."

"Well, you know how much I enjoy your conversation, Soph." Jess grinned. "Tell us all about that imported water again?"

"The shower isn't working," she said to me, ignoring Jess. "Go and complain to the manager and get him to send someone up."

"Are you sure it's not working?" I asked.

"Have you tried turning it on?" Jess added.

"Of course I tried turning it on!" Sophie spat. "Can you just go and get someone?"

"Let me see if I can fix it," I offered, continuing on my quest to get along with my temporary roommate.

Jess raised her eyebrows as I strode into the bathroom and pretended I knew what I was doing. I twiddled the tap handles of the bath backward and forward, but nothing happened so I pulled the showerhead from its stand to inspect it. "Maybe it is broken."

"No kidding," Sophie snarled, snatching the showerhead from me and inspecting it herself while I twiddled the tap some more. "I told you it was broken."

I turned the cold tap as far as it would go and then pulled out the latch in the middle of the taps as an experiment. Suddenly there was a low rumble and the shower burst into life, water shooting out of the showerhead at full force and straight into Sophie's face.

She screamed and dropped the showerhead, but with the water flowing through the pipe it took on a life of its own and flung itself around wildly as I tried to catch it. Unfortunately, my catching skills are on the same level as a penguin's so I was just sort of leaping around as the showerhead flew around the room, soaking the bathroom, Sophie, and myself.

"STOP TRYING TO CATCH IT! TURN IT OFF, YOU MORON!" Sophie screamed. I lurched toward the tap, turning it off as quickly as possible. We both stood in silence, dripping wet, while Jess howled in laughter having witnessed the whole scene from the comfortable front-row seat of my bed.

"That was kind of fun. Right?" I suggested, looking at Sophie hopefully, water dripping down my face.

She gripped her sopping towel, her sodden hair slapped flat against her head.

"Maybe not so fun," I mumbled, reading her angry expression, which, interestingly, reminded me a little of Darth Vader's mask. I decided not to tell her that, though.

"This is going to be a *disaster*," Sophie hissed, pointing at the doorway to instruct my exit from the bathroom. She slammed the door behind me.

Jess wiped away her tears of laughter and threw a towel at me. "Hilarious. You two should have your own show."

9.

From: connorlawrence1@zingmail.co.uk
To: anna_huntley@zingmail.co.uk
Subject: Hey!

Hey, Spidey!

Sorry I missed your call—I keep my phone on silent when I'm drawing—but glad you got there safe and sound. I was going to call back, but by the time I saw your missed call it was really late, and considering you're sharing with She Who Must Not Be Named, I figured I better not risk awakening the beast.

Such bad luck on the room share—did you ask Mrs. Ginnwell if you could swap?

So, have you eaten your weight in gelato yet? I guess you only just arrived so that would be impressive. Make sure you hunt down a store that has a Nutella flavor. I know they do that out there. You should start a campaign to get them to import Nutella ice cream from Italy to England! With your It Girl status I bet you could make it happen.

I'm all good. Have been working today on the storyline and just sketching out some ideas. I need to think of a bad guy and sidekick for this one. Maybe I can ask Sophie and Josie to pose for me? Just kidding. I could never spend that long in a room with either of them.

Have a brilliant time and call me if you get the chance. I want to hear all about your first day seeing the sights.

Connor xx

"Morning, brainiac. What are you reading?"

"Hey!" I yelped as Jess snatched the piece of paper from my hand when she found me waiting for her on the stairs.

She glanced at the first few lines as she strode past, with me tripping down the steps behind her. "Is this an e-mail from Connor?" She smiled mischievously, handing it back to me. "And you printed it out because?"

"Because," I huffed, grabbing it from her hand, "I didn't have time to read it before breakfast."

Jess snorted. "You are such a bad liar. You wanted to study it, didn't you?"

"What do you think it means if he put two kisses on the end? That's a good sign, right? Or do you think he should have put more than two?"

"I think it's a good sign." Jess yawned as we made our way toward the breakfast room.

"But he doesn't say anything about missing me," I said, scanning the e-mail again. "Is that a bad sign?"

"It's been *one* night."

"I suppose you're right. But do you think it's bad that he didn't call? I mean, I gave him the number to call. But then he was working all day so maybe he didn't see my message. And he does say he *would* have called, but he didn't want to wake Sophie, which is very sensible of him. But then he could have called this morning. Do you think if he actually missed me he would have called this morning?"

"I think it's too early to deal with your crazy."

"Maybe I should call him. Do you think I should call him? He does say I should call him. But I think he means this evening rather than this morning. Here, what do you think?" I passed Jess the piece of paper again, anxious for her opinion.

She took it from me, screwed it up into a ball, and tossed it into the trash can.

"OI! What did you do that for?" I whined as we approached the breakfast buffet.

"Because, Anna, we're in *Rome*. It's our vacation. That means you need to relax and just enjoy it."

"Yeah," I sighed. "I just wish he was here too, to enjoy it with us."

"I know. We all wish that. But no more studying every letter of his e-mails. Otherwise you'll just read things into them that aren't there." Jess placed a hand on my shoulder. "Of course he misses you. Who wouldn't?"

I smiled up at her. Despite the constant ribbing, Jess always had the knack of making me feel better.

"Come on. Let's go join the others," she said, moving over to join Danny and Stephanie, who were on their own at one of the tables, studying Danny's guidebook.

"Good morning," Stephanie said chirpily, looking up from the book as we sat down. "How did you guys sleep?

"Not well," Jess groaned, resting her head in her hand and stirring her yogurt. "Josie kept thinking she heard something so she turned the light on and off, like, a hundred times."

Danny, Stephanie, and I all looked across the breakfast tables toward Josie, who was talking loudly about her belief that the hotel was haunted.

"She is ridiculous," Stephanie said sympathetically.

"She's the worst!" Jess whispered.

"Er, actually, I beg to differ. I think Sophie Parker is the worst," I replied, having suffered greatly at the hands of Madame Queen Bee so far on this trip.

Reasons why sharing a room with Sophie Parker for two weeks is The Worst and will end with everlasting psychological trauma:

> 1. Do you know how I was woken on my first day in Rome? BY CHOKING.
> Yes, that's right, choking. Sophie was using so much hairspray that it filled the entire room—and my lungs. I woke up coughing through the haze before running to the window and throwing it open so I could get some fresh oxygen. She didn't even apologize and continued to

spray every tiny strand into place. What happens if next time I don't wake up? EVER?

2. Instead of saying "Good morning," she offers nonconstructive criticism.

Like when I stopped spluttering after she tried choking me with hairspray fumes and she said, "You so do NOT look cute when you're sleeping." This made me not want to fall asleep ever again.

3. She uses all the towels when she showers.

Seriously, ALL the towels. I was left with a hand towel to work with, which covered precisely nothing. When I mentioned this politely after I'd had to ask her to pass my clothes through from the bedroom as I couldn't come out wearing a WASHCLOTH, she just shrugged and went, "Yeah, but I need that many towels. Deal with it."

WHO IS THIS MONSTER?

4. I will never survive two weeks of her BRUTALLY honest comments like these ones:

"Really? That's what you're wearing? But it's awful."

"I don't like your hair up."

"Your hair down looks flat."

"Don't you think you should wear more makeup?"

"No. More makeup than *that* even."

"I was thinking last night about that weird lecture you gave me about bugs. It made me wonder whether you're completely socially inept or whether you're an actual freak."

"Nice try, but I still think I win in the worst-roommate stakes," Jess insisted. "At least yours let you have some sleep. I feel like death. Why do we have to be up at this hour anyway?"

"We're going to Vatican City today," Danny said excitedly, grabbing Stephanie's hand. "There's bound to be a line so we have to get there early."

Stephanie chuckled and looked at Danny adoringly as he practically bounced in his seat. I looked down at my breakfast, not wanting to let on how envious I was that I didn't have Connor here to get excited with.

"Well, thanks to my roommate's overactive imagination I'll probably be too tired to care about anything I see today," Jess huffed.

"At least she doesn't poison you with hairspray," I reasoned.

"And I forgot to mention that Sophie said that my outfit reminded her of an ice cream."

"That might be a nice thing," Danny pointed out through a mouthful of cereal.

"Sure. In another universe where Sophie says nice things to me."

"They've done this on purpose," Jess said, slamming down her spoon and narrowing her eyes at the teachers as they came in. "It's some kind of messed-up plot to make us all hate the trip and feel grateful to be back at school come September."

"We're going to have a good time on this trip," Danny said firmly as Stephanie squeezed him around the waist support-ively. "Regardless of crazy conspiracy theories."

Jess narrowed her eyes at him.

The teachers rounded us up in the hotel reception area after breakfast, counted our heads, and then ushered us outside. Mrs. Ginnwell led the charge, holding up her Union Jack flag, and walking ahead of us to where the coach was parked, like a duck proudly escorting her line of ducklings.

I don't know whether it was because I had been so tired from the flight the day before or the shock of being told I would be sharing a room with Sophie, but somehow I had totally missed how beautiful the street we were staying on was.

It was just like I had stepped into that old film Dad made me watch once—A *Room with a View*—except I wasn't carrying a frilly parasol and there were no naked men running around a lake. But, still, it was totally similar—the sun was shining down on the tall stone buildings lining the cobbled street, and all the window sills had these cute flowerpots on them.

"Really pretty, isn't it?" came a voice from behind me.

I turned around, startled. "Er, yes, James. And that's a very in-touch-with-your-feelings way of describing it," I said, raising an eyebrow skeptically.

"Didn't mean to make you jump." He grinned. "You want to come get on the bus before you get left behind or should I give you some more time with the really pretty walls?"

"Haha."

"Come on, you two!" Mr. Kenton yelled. "We've got a lot to see and not much time in which to see it."

"So, are you going to talk about the fact that you reduced the London Comic Con to rubble the other day or are we pretending that it didn't happen?" James said, as we walked quickly to catch up with the rest of the group. "Not bad destruction skills for such a small person."

"Reducing it to rubble is a slight exaggeration," I huffed.

"I think, personally, it's impressive that you can bring an entire event to a standstill. You should be proud at how good you're getting at standing out."

"Ha! I'd much rather blend in."

James laughed. "Not much chance of that happening, Anna Huntley."

Not quite sure how to respond to that, I was halfway to whacking him around the head when we got ushered onto the bus by Mrs. Ginnwell. I jumped into the seat next to Jess in front of Danny and Stephanie, and James slid in next to Brendan across the aisle.

"Here we go!" Danny said, leaning his face into the gap between our seats as the bus rumbled into action. "Jess, make sure you get some good pictures of all the architecture."

Jess twisted in her seat, held the lens of her amazing state-of-the-art camera up to Danny's face, and clicked, the flash making him lurch back in surprise.

Ever since Jess had won an internship at a fashion magazine, she'd been really into her photography and had done the best art project of anyone in the school at the end of last semester, so it didn't surprise anyone that most of her luggage was made up of expensive photography equipment.

"Well, that's a keeper," she announced, squinting at the

screen as Stephanie and I giggled and Danny rubbed his eyes. "I do love a close-up."

"My vision is all blotchy now!" Danny whined.

"Well, then don't tell me what to do in the future when it comes to photography."

"I didn't realize you were such a sensitive artist," Danny sighed.

"I have a vision," Jess said, sitting upright and putting on a husky, dramatic voice.

"Hey, Jess!" Brendan knelt up on his seat. "Get a photo of me and Tyndale." He threw an arm around James, and then stuck out his tongue. "Or perhaps you would prefer a different pose so you can see some muscle," Brendan added, raising one eyebrow and flexing his arms. "Watch out, ladies."

"Sit down, you idiot." James laughed, pushing Brendan back into his seat.

"Brendan, you're such a show-off," said Sophie, who was leaning over the seat behind Brendan slightly possessively.

"Hey, look at this," Josie said loudly, desperately trying to get Sophie's attention by flapping a magazine in her face. "Apparently Marianne Montaine and Tom Kyzer have broken up. Maybe Tom dumped her after seeing her in this dress," Josie cackled, looking over at me.

I stared out of the window, feeling my cheeks growing hot, trying to ignore her. My breath caught for a moment in panic before I reminded myself of the time a gossip magazine had announced my plans for a solo album in collaboration with Cliff Richard—it was just another lie. I'd come here to get away from all that, and I didn't want to give Josie the satisfaction of paying her any attention.

Sophie glanced at it but just went, "I like that dress," dismissively, studying her nails as if it were all beneath her.

"Yeah, I mean, I guess it's nice," Josie said quickly, crestfallen, before trying another tack. "Maybe it's her *family* that has been putting him off. How embarrassing for her."

"They haven't broken up," I blurted out, indignation boiling up inside me.

"It says here they've been arguing about each other's party habits too and have grown apart," Josie read pompously. "That relationship didn't last long, did it?"

"I think we'll believe what Anna, Marianne's future stepsister who hangs out with her all the time, says over some random journalist who has never met them." Jess snickered.

"Some of these articles are true!" Josie squeaked, her cheeks going bright red. "Celebrities break up all the time!"

"I'm sure," I said, trying to stay calm just like Connor

would have told me to, "but I can tell you that Marianne and Tom are definitely not breaking up. In fact, they're moving in together."

"Guys!" Danny cried. "We're here! And you've missed all the beautiful sights on the way. Steph, pass me the guidebook. Anna, would you like to hear some interesting facts about Vatican City?"

"I would love to," I said, clambering off the bus as fast as I could and out into the sun.

As Danny began reeling off facts that I wasn't paying any attention to, I put on my sunglasses and took in the towering city walls and the line that was building alongside it.

"Come on, boys and girls!" Miss Lawler said excitedly, leading us to join it.

Danny followed eagerly, breaking away from me to talk to Stephanie, and I found myself walking dismally next to Josie.

"Never mind Tom Kyzer and Marianne Montaine," she began, clearly annoyed to have been proven wrong in front of everyone a moment ago. "Where's *your* boyfriend, Anna?"

"Connor is focusing on his comic book," I informed her proudly. "You know his first one got published? He's working on his second one now."

"Really? That's strange." She feigned concern. "You'd

think when he's got the whole summer to work on it, he might want to spend two weeks with his new girlfriend. You have only just gotten together, haven't you? He must be *very* dedicated."

"He is," I said uncomfortably.

"Amazing that your family's . . . situation hasn't scared him off, isn't it?"

"I don't know what you're talking about, Josie," I sighed, looking around for someone to help me escape from her, but Jess was busy instructing Stephanie to stand a certain way so she could get a good shot of her outside the Vatican while Danny had drifted a way off to converse with Miss Lawler about the construction of the medieval walls.

Josie cackled. "No privacy, disastrous first dates splashed all over the newspapers . . . personally I wouldn't like it, but I guess everyone is different."

"There you are, Josie," came a voice behind us. We both spun around to find James standing there, rubbing the lenses of his sunglasses on his T-shirt. "Sophie is looking for you. She said something about a lip gloss emergency?"

Josie snapped to attention, reaching quickly into her bag and holding up a lip gloss triumphantly. "Thanks so much, Jayjay. I'll go sort it out."

Looking proud to be called on for such an important mission, she hurriedly tottered off down the line in search of her Queen Bee.

I grinned. "Thanks for that, Jayjay."

"Call me Jayjay again and I won't be rescuing you next time."

From: anna_huntley@zingmail.co.uk
To: connorlawrence1@zingmail.co.uk
Subject: Greetings from Rome!
Hey!
Thanks so much for your e-mail last night! How is the comic book going today? Did you have a good morning?
I'm just in an Internet café near the Vatican—we went there this morning and it was amazing.
I was all prepared to meet the pope but according to Danny he doesn't wander around all day talking to tourists, so that was kind of disappointing.
I wish you were here, especially this morning when Josie showed us all the stupid magazines she'd got at the airport. She was

saying all these things about Marianne, which totally aren't true. You always know what to do in those situations.

But, you know, apart from that, it has been an amazing day so far! I better go as Jess is complaining about how hot it is in here. Talk to you later?

Anna xx

10.

From: anna_huntley@zingmail.co.uk
To: marianne@montaines.co.uk;
rebecca.blythe@bounce-mail.co.uk;
helena@montaines.co.uk
Subject: Rome
Hi Mom, Helena, and Marianne,
Went to the Sistine Chapel today. That was
cool. Hope you're good.
Love, me xxx

From: marianne@montaines.co.uk
To: helena@montaines.co.uk;
anna_huntley@zingmail.co.uk;
rebecca.blythe@bounce-mail.co.uk
Subject: Re: Rome

Thanks for that, Anna. It's like we were there.
Marianne x

From: rebecca.blythe@bounce-mail.co.uk
To: marianne@montaines.co.uk;
helena@montaines.co.uk;
anna_huntley@zingmail.co.uk
Subject: Re: Rome
Darling,
I must say you really have a flair for travel
writing. Such thorough and detailed
description!
Of course, you didn't have a lot to work
with. It's not as though the Sistine Chapel
is one of the most celebrated and beautiful
masterpieces in the world with a ceiling
painted by the great artist Michelangelo,
featuring several poignant scenes from
the Old Testament, taking him five years
to complete, along with wall paintings and
tapestries created by many other leading
painters of the time.

It may have taken a lot of blood, sweat, and tears, but those artists of the fifteenth century can rest in peace knowing that you have visited such a haven and emerged with wisdom and a way with words beyond your fourteen years: "That was cool." It shall be quoted for years to come!

Mom xxx

From: helena@montaines.co.uk
To: marianne@montaines.co.uk;
anna_huntley@zingmail.co.uk;
rebecca.blythe@bounce-mail.co.uk
Subject: Re: Rome

Dearest Rebecca,

How you astound me with your incredible knowledge! I feel I have learned so much from your e-mail. I believe I visited the Sistine Chapel myself a decade ago when I was in Italy promoting a dreadful film that I was in—a film no one has ever heard of, thank goodness— about men running around in shorts.

Helena x

From: rebecca.blythe@bounce-mail.co.uk
To: marianne@montaines.co.uk;
helena@montaines.co.uk;
anna_huntley@zingmail.co.uk
Subject: Re: Rome
Helena, you are too kind! I am sure you are
being modest. How did your appointment with
Fenella go this morning?
Rebecca x

PS A film about men running around in
shorts doesn't sound dreadful in the least!
It sounds like something I'd greatly enjoy
watching.

From: helena@montaines.co.uk
To: marianne@montaines.co.uk;
anna_huntley@zingmail.co.uk;
rebecca.blythe@bounce-mail.co.uk
Subject: Re: Rome
Oh, how sweet of you to remember! We were
discussing pants. I must tell you all about it.
Helena x

PS Let me assure you, it was quite the bore. Men kept talking about a mug and the camera zooms in on me looking distressed a few times, but you can hardly see my expression through the perm. I can't even remember what it's called.

From: rebecca.blythe@bounce-mail.co.uk
To: marianne@montaines.co.uk;
helena@montaines.co.uk;
anna_huntley@zingmail.co.uk
Subject: Re: Rome
A film about men running around in shorts and talking about mugs? Sounds very trendy!
Do tell us about the pants.
Rebecca x

From: marianne@montaines.co.uk
To: helena@montaines.co.uk;
anna_huntley@zingmail.co.uk;
rebecca.blythe@bounce-mail.co.uk
Subject: Re: Rome

I don't want to be part of the discussion about pants.

And, Mom, that film was about an underdog team winning the FIFA World Cup. Not a mug. A WORLD CUP.

Thank God only about two people ever saw it . . .

Marianne x

From: helena@montaines.co.uk
To: marianne@montaines.co.uk;
anna_huntley@zingmail.co.uk;
rebecca.blythe@bounce-mail.co.uk
Subject: Re: Rome

I tried on several pants, Rebecca, but I just wasn't quite sure of the style. Some of the ones I tried on were simply enormous! To hold everything in, you know.

One of the pairs I was quite sure were going to engulf me completely and I would never be seen again, forever lost in a pair of pants, but they turned out to be very nifty when it came to the stomach area.

Helena x

From: rebecca.blythe@bounce-mail.co.uk
To: marianne@montaines.co.uk;
helena@montaines.co.uk;
anna_huntley@zingmail.co.uk
Subject: Re: Rome
The pants experience sounds almost traumatic, Helena! I once had a similar experience in China when I mistook a local sumo wrestler's pants for my own after a bathing session.
Rebecca x

From: helena@montaines.co.uk
To: marianne@montaines.co.uk;
anna_huntley@zingmail.co.uk;
rebecca.blythe@bounce-mail.co.uk
Subject: Re: Rome
Those pants must have been at least five times your size, Rebecca! Whatever did you do?
Helena x

From: rebecca.blythe@bounce-mail.co.uk
To: marianne@montaines.co.uk;

helena@montaines.co.uk;
anna_huntley@zingmail.co.uk
Subject: Re: Rome

I will have to tell you all about it over dinner, Helena, as the end of the story involved a chance meeting with Matthew Cornes, a young man who I determined must fall in love with me. In the end it turned out we were very incompatible due to his obsession with lizards, but it really is quite the tale. All thanks to a pair of Chinese sumo wrestler's pants!

Matthew owns a delightful restaurant in the West End these days. We should go there, Helena! Wonderful tapas.

Rebecca x

From: helena@montaines.co.uk
To: marianne@montaines.co.uk;
anna_huntley@zingmail.co.uk;
rebecca.blythe@bounce-mail.co.uk
Subject: Re: Rome

I would love to visit the restaurant of this lizard

fellow! I simply love tapas. All those little plates are so adorable.

You can finish telling me the sumo-wrestler-pants story when we go. I'm dying to know! Then I can tell you about the time as a teenager I got into a bit of trouble with a lawn mower while trying to impress the rugged gardener who worked at our house.

Helena x

From: anna_huntley@zingmail.co.uk
To: marianne@montaines.co.uk;
rebecca.blythe@bounce-mail.co.uk;
helena@montaines.co.uk
Subject: Re: Rome

As ever, thank you for this insightful chain of messages.

With you two as our guiding lights, it is a miracle that Marianne and I have not ended up in prison.

Love, me xxx

11.

MOMENTS IN MY LIFE WHEN I'VE BEEN PUT IN charge of a project that didn't turn out as planned:

1. The time Dad said I could be in charge of putting up the Christmas tree lights and then I got tangled in all the stupid wires and he had to cut me out with his pliers.

If you ask me, I did him a favor. It was about time he made the effort to go buy some new lights rather than using ones that were so old they may have actually been present in the stable at Bethlehem, providing light for Mary and Joseph.

2. The time Dad said I could be in charge of carving the roast lamb and I dropped it on the floor. Clearly SOMEONE hadn't cooked it very well if

it slipped off the plate that easily. And it wasn't MY fault that Dog then stole the lamb, ate a chunk of it, and threw up on Dad's antique chess set. I don't know why Dad was so angry; we hadn't been able to use the chess set anyway ever since Dog ate three pawns and a bishop.

3. The time Mom said I could be in charge of the car while she popped into the shop and then I locked myself in and her out.

I blame it on her stupid high-tech keys that have all these buttons that you press. There was no use in her yelling "CLICK UNLOCK!" through the window at me either because I had no idea which button that one was.

4. The time when Mom said I could be in charge of ordering the food in a restaurant in Paris to practice my French and instead of saying to the waiter "Thanks a lot" at the end of my order, I said "Thank you nice bottom."

French is stupid.

5. The time when the teachers put me in charge of ringing this big old fashioned bell as part of a school tradition during the school's birthday

and I hit myself in the face with the bell and knocked myself out.

There were some serious health and safety issues here. It's a miracle I didn't sue the school. Lucky for them I'm a very forgiving human being.

6. The time in Rome when I was put in charge of my group's map and we ended up completely lost in the middle of an excavation site with a load of stray cats looking at us.

"Who put Anna in charge of the map?" Josie wailed, after shooing away a particularly curious cat.

"We all have to take turns and it was Anna's," Jess explained, crouching down in her denim shorts with her camera to get a good shot of all the cats. "I think this is really cool. It's like the less-explored non-tourist part of Rome."

"Yeah, there's a *reason* why this part isn't explored," Josie huffed. "Can someone PLEASE tell this cat to GO AWAY."

"It's just a cat." James rolled his eyes. "Relax, Josie. Anna will lead us in the right direction."

"Miss Lawler," Josie whined. "Can't you just tell us where to go?"

"I'm as clueless as you are," replied Miss Lawler. She shrugged happily, straightening her sun hat and admiring her surroundings. "Plus, we're not meant to help you with these tasks. We're here to observe."

"Urgh! I wish Sophie was here!"

"What, so she could do the whining while you just nod along?" Jess asked, clicking away as Josie seethed. "Enjoy the freedom away from your master, Josie. You can actually have your own opinion without checking it's the right one with her first."

"I think we need to go this way!" I said, pointing down a narrow road to our right enthusiastically, and trying to look as though I knew what I was doing.

"Great!" Jess got to her feet. "Good going, Anna."

As she gave me a big thumbs-up, I felt such relief at having her in a group with me. At first I had really panicked when Mrs. Ginnwell had announced that we would be spending the majority of the trip split into groups with a list of tasks to complete each day so that we would "get the most out of this intellectually stimulating and illuminative trip." She had started reading out the list of names for Group 1 and Stephanie's name was called out right after Sophie's. Stephanie gulped so loud that it echoed around the breakfast room.

I practically whooped when she moved on to Group 2

and I could rest safe in the knowledge that Sophie and I would only be sharing evenings with each other and not daytime too.

Danny was put in Group 3 and his eyebrows furrowed as the other names in his group were called out.

"What's wrong?" I asked. "Your group isn't too bad."

"None of you are in it." He shrugged, causing Stephanie to go "aw" and peck him on the cheek.

I wondered if Connor would have been in my group if he had been here.

"Don't worry, Dan," Jess said, picking up his hand and cradling it in hers. "I'm sure everyone in your group will appreciate your lectures as much as we do. The one you gave us yesterday on the history of Vatican City thrilled me to the core. That King Julian guy did an excellent job sorting out that whole Brazilian situation."

"Pope Julius II," Danny corrected through gritted teeth, pulling his hand free, "and it's St. Peter's *Basilica*, not Brazilian!"

Mrs. Ginnwell moved on to Group 4, which was made up of everyone who hadn't been called out yet, including myself and Jess, who winked at me as Mrs. Ginnwell announced both our names, but then did a gagging motion as Josie's name was read out.

Josie aside, my group was quite a good one, and although I was sad that we wouldn't be going around the city completing all the tasks with Danny and Stephanie, I would have Jess next to me, and James was with us too.

"I think you're right, Anna," James said, pointing at the map and interrupting my chain of thought. "We must have just taken a wrong turn at some point."

"And ended up in the land of cats." Josie scowled, pushing her large black sunglasses up her delicate nose. "Gross."

"I told you guys I shouldn't be put in charge of the map. Maybe you should take over, Jess," I suggested hopefully, holding it out for her.

Miss Lawler jumped in. "No, no, Anna, your turn isn't up yet. It's a very important life skill and it's all part of the fun."

Josie let out a loud "HA!" and then under her breath went, "Some fun THIS is," kicking the dust out of her sandal and straightening her far-too-short summer dress.

Miss Lawler ignored her. "Lead the way then, Anna. Soon we'll all be at the church of Santa Maria in Cosmedin, and you will be amazed at the wonders and delights you will discover there. The interiors are really quite something."

James smirked at me as Josie made a face that plainly showed she couldn't care less about the interiors of a church.

But there was something inside this one that I was really excited to see.

We finally made it to the church and I wandered in, stopping among the beautiful wooden pews to take it all in, awestruck by the peacefulness.

"It's not bad, huh? Guess Miss Lawler was right about those interiors," James whispered. My eyes scanned the ancient columns and archways. "What are you looking for?" he asked. I gasped when I spotted what I was after and he followed my eyeline. "Whoa, what *is* that? It's massive!"

"Here," I told him, dragging him toward a large, round sculpture. "*La Bocca della Verità.*"

I gestured for Jess to come and join us and pointed at the face of a man carved into the large marble stone, his mouth a big gaping hole. "You have to take a picture of me next to this!"

"It's kind of creepy," Jess observed, and then grinned at me. "Is there a reason why you look like you've just won the lottery? It could be the heat, but you're practically glowing."

"Guys, this is extremely famous. You haven't heard of it?"

They both looked at me blankly. "The story goes that if you put your hand in his mouth and told a lie, your hand would get bitten off."

"Right," Jess nodded. "That's even more creepy."

"But more importantly, it is in a famous moment of cinematic history!" I enthused.

"Ah, that's why you've heard of it, Film Geek." Jess grinned.

"Not too loud, Anna," Miss Lawler hushed, coming over to us. "Ah, I see you've found the *Bocca della Verità*. This sculpture might have been part of an ancient fountain, I believe. Beautiful, isn't it?"

"You guys know the film *Roman Holiday*, right? With Gregory Peck and Audrey Hepburn?"

Jess and James looked at me blankly but Miss Lawler nodded, smiling. "It's one of my favorites."

"Is this one of your weird old movies that you go on about?" Jess asked.

"Gregory Peck is a reporter and he's hanging out with Audrey Hepburn, who is a princess, but they're both lying about who they are. Anyway, they come to this very church!" At this point I was so excited I was practically hopping up and down on the spot. "And then Gregory Peck tells her about putting your hand in this sculpture's mouth and the tale about it being bitten off. Then he pretends suddenly that his hand is bitten off and she screams! It's a really famous scene!"

"Well, this will make a great picture. Anna and James, put

your hands in and pretend they're getting bitten off."

Jess lifted her camera as we both stepped forward, ready to slide our hands into the gaping marble hole. I made a face and hunched slightly as though in great pain, and after he'd finished laughing at me—"You look like you're trying to be a gargoyle"—James did his own version too.

"Now put them all the way in so you can say that you've done it!" Jess urged.

We leaned forward, and James squeezed in his hand. His skin was warm next to mine in the cold stone hole. I looked up at him, ready to take the cue for our next silly faces but he was actually looking down at me, very intently.

Jess's camera clicked.

And suddenly James jerked back and pulled his hand away. "Sorry."

"That's okay!" I laughed, a bit confused. "Do I have cold hands?"

"Terrible circulation," he confirmed, nodding mock seriously.

"Perfect!" Jess announced, examining the shot on her camera's display screen.

"A real movie moment," Miss Lawler sighed. "And who

knows the English translation for *Bocca della Verità?*"

I did. "The Mouth of Truth."

From: anna_huntley@zingmail.co.uk
To: connorlawrence1@zingmail.co.uk
Subject: Me again!

Hi, did you get my message yesterday? Maybe there was something wrong with that stupid Internet café and it didn't get to you. . . . The computers did look as though they had been bought in the Stone Age!

So, anyway, today was fun. . . . Me, Jess, Josie (unfortunately), and James saw the *Bocca della Verità*—you know, the sculpture that's in *Roman Holiday*!!

I was so excited but no one else was that bothered about the whole movie link. If only you'd been there!

I was in charge of the map for a bit and got us completely lost but that was kind of fun too, like a weird adventure. Jess has taken a BILLION photos so you'll be able to see loads when we get back.

How's the comic book coming along? Any developments?

Missing you xx

From: connorlawrence1@zingmail.co.uk
To: anna_huntley@zingmail.co.uk
Subject: Re: Me again!

Hi Anna, I'm sorry I didn't get back to you right away, the craziest thing has happened. . . .

An agent contacted me today. AN AGENT. Can you believe it? That means that they think I have potential, right?

They said that it didn't matter that I was still at school, that my age might even work in my favor as a good selling point! They said, and I quote, that they think I have a "great future in the graphic-novel world."

Can you believe it? My mom is taking me out for a big meal tonight to celebrate so I've got to rush off, but I wanted you to be one of the first to know. After all, you inspired the whole thing. Wish you could be here to celebrate with me!

> Great you had a good day—I hope James and
> Josie weren't too cliquey. Can't wait to see all
> Jess's photos when you're back. You been to
> the Trevi Fountain yet? Be sure to make a good
> wish. . . .
> Connor
> X

He meant us, right? A good wish about us? That means a LOT. It completely cancels out that he only put one kiss this time. Not that I'm reading into stupid stuff like that. And, without saying it, he definitely implies that he misses me too: *Wish you could be here to celebrate with me!*

That means WAY more than the fact he hadn't had time to e-mail me back.

12.

When Anna's in Rome!

By Nancy Rose—*Daily Post*

Fresh from her Comic Con drama, it seems British It Girl Anna Huntley is not content to lie low for long, as she's been spotted out and about having fun with friends on the streets of Rome, the *Daily Post* can reveal. Despite rumors that the young socialite has been dating the young man from her school with whom she was spotted at Comic Con earlier this month, Anna—the teenage daughter of journalist Nick Huntley, due to marry actress Helena Montaine this summer—has since been seen enjoying Italy without him. Showing her fun side, the young It Girl was photographed jumping out from behind Italian landmarks in an attempt to scare her friends. "Anna deserves a break," a source close to the family can reveal. "She has had a difficult few weeks and needed to get away from her critics." By the look of the smile on her face, the sun-kissed Anna has put her troubles behind her! When in Rome!

"You jumped out at Josie . . . from a tomb?"

My dad sounded puzzled on the phone. I'd just been getting ready to go down to breakfast when he called to read out the reports that were being printed in the English press about me.

"My personal favorite has to be the one Marianne e-mailed me. Here, listen to this part: 'Often under the watch of her strict father at home, Anna has been given the opportunity to spread her wings abroad.'"

"At least they've got one fact right."

"I hope you're not referring to the strict-dad comment," he said, clearing his throat. "So, your taste of freedom involves frightening the life out of girls in your class?"

"We were at the burial site of Keats and Shelley."

"A perfect opportunity for practical jokes . . ."

"It wasn't planned! And I didn't realize anyone was taking photos."

"Continue."

"Well, our task was to find what's written on their stones

and so on and so forth, and Josie was going on about how her idea of a vacation was not going to a boring cemetery. Anyway, I mentioned to James—you know James—that I felt that Josie was starting to upset Miss Lawler a bit because, you know, Miss Lawler's so enthusiastic and she looked so down when Josie wouldn't stop complaining. She's been complaining nonstop for DAYS. So James thought it might be fun to try to make Josie smile. You know, get her to lighten up and stop spoiling it for everyone else."

"And his idea to make Josie 'lighten up' was to jump out from a tomb and give her a heart attack?"

"It was hilarious, Dad, honestly," I giggled. "I wish Jess had gotten a photo of Josie's expression. She screamed so loudly I thought my eardrums had burst! But it was worth it just to see her face."

"I can imagine. I'm pleased you're letting your hair down, Anna, as long as you're not getting into trouble."

"I promise I'm not. James and Josie are friends so she did laugh in the end. James gave her a big hug and she just relaxed. It worked! Miss Lawler was grateful, not angry. I don't think Josie will be very happy with me this morning though."

"I can't imagine why."

"It's actually nothing to do with the tomb. Last night we went to learn circus skills with Italian performers—seriously, Dad, the teachers have gone all out to make sure we experience *everything* here—and it turns out that I'm not a natural when it comes to spinning plates."

"Please don't tell me that I need to send apology flowers to Josie's parents *again*?" He groaned.

"No, I didn't set her on fire or hit her in the face," I said proudly. "But I did almost take her head off with a plate when it flew off toward her. She's getting better at ducking! Anyway, she stood up straight and went, "STOP. TRYING. TO. KILL. ME." It was terrifying, but everyone else found it hilarious. Well, Jess, Danny, and Stephanie anyway."

"Poor Josie." Dad laughed.

"And Jess got a good picture of me doing the Hula-Hoop. I could actually do that one."

"Let's hope that doesn't get in the press. I hope no one is bothering you too much."

"Hardly at all." I yawned, fiddling with the coils of the phone cord. "Like I said, I didn't even notice people taking photos of me at the tomb."

"Now there's one, though, more will follow. Just be aware, okay?"

"Sure. You okay, Dad? You sound kind of . . . serious all of a sudden."

"Yeah, I'm okay. We haven't been having an easy time of it here, if I'm honest with you, Anna-pops." He sighed.

"What's wrong?" I sat up straight, panicking. "Is it Dog? Did he eat another set of keys again?"

"No, no, Dog is fine. It's to do with the wedding."

"The wedding?" I physically relaxed. "Dad, stop worrying. It will be fine. Fenella has got it all under control."

"I'm not so sure. The press are following me *everywhere*. I can't do one blooming thing without them shouting in my face. It has become very intense. It's making me not want to leave the house."

"It was always going to be worse around the wedding," I said, my stomach tightening at how down he sounded, and trying not to think about Josie's gloating on celebrity relationships. "You've just got to get on with things as normal. That's what you always tell me, right?"

"Yes, you're right, of course," he agreed, suddenly sounding more Dad-like and practical. "When did you get so wise? Anyway, you don't worry about it and have a wonderful time out there, okay?"

"Okay, Dad. Are you sure you're all right?"

"Absolutely," he stated firmly. "We'll talk later. Everything is fine."

We said good-bye and I put the phone down, feeling uneasy. I wasn't sure if he had really been trying to persuade me that everything was fine—or persuading himself.

"You're not coming tonight? But we're making spaghetti!" James shook his head at me, bewildered. "Why would you want to miss making spaghetti in Italy? It's where spaghetti comes from!"

"I know, but I really need to phone my dad back and talk to him about something—"

"What kind of phone call needs a whole evening? Phone him before we go and then come make spaghetti, bonehead," Jess chuckled, picking up a bright orange-colored vegetable from one of the stands. "What even *is* this?"

We were wandering up and down hundreds of rows of colorful market stalls in bustling Campo de' Fiori where people were selling vegetables, fruit, spices, flowers, plants, and even fish. Jess was in her element, taking photos of stallholders at work with their stands overflowing with produce, going on about the spectrum of colors she was capturing.

"I don't know. He just wasn't himself earlier and I felt like he rushed me off the phone," I reasoned as she put the vegetable down and picked up another one to inspect.

"Of course he's not himself—he's getting married to the most famous actress in the world!" Jess shook her head. "That's going to mess with your head."

"He doesn't see her as the most famous actress in the world. She's just Helena."

"Yeah, obviously, but think about it." She shrugged. "People get crazy in the lead-up to their weddings and he's got the added pressure of the whole world watching."

"It sounds like you're worrying too much," James declared, swinging a string of garlic around to make us laugh until the vendor asked him to stop. At least, we think he asked him to stop. We actually had no idea what he was saying, but there were a lot of frenzied hand gestures, so James placed the garlic down carefully and backed away. "Like Jess said," he continued, "he's probably just a bit stressed about the wedding."

"He's been stressed about the wedding before." I sighed. "Trust me, he sounded different this time. I just want to check that he's not . . . panicking."

"What, you think he's going to cancel the wedding?" Jess blew a raspberry. "Don't be stupid, Anna. He's crazy in love with Helena. I mean, no offense, but they're kind of gross about it." She took a photo of a row of buckets exploding with colorful flowers.

"Of course not," I said, my brow furrowing. "He would never do that to Helena. But he said that there've been so many photographers following him around he doesn't like leaving the house. That doesn't sound like my dad. I just want to talk to him properly."

"Well, do what you need to do," Jess said, clapping me on the back. "On one condition."

"Yes?"

"After your phone call and after we've finished making spaghetti, we meet up and go and get some ice cream. We need to get away from the teachers so that you can get an Italian boy to ask me out," Jess said determinedly.

"You need Anna's help in getting boys to ask you out?" James smiled mischievously.

"No, I mean that I—oh my goodness, would you look at the SIZE of this avocado?!—I mean that I could use some of Anna's fame advantage."

"What's fame advantage?"

"Oh, you know, Anna and I are out walking and some handsome Italian men recognize her so they ask for her picture and then we get chatting and it turns out that they happen to have some Vespas and they would love to take us to see the sights on them," she said dreamily. "Or, even better, Anna could get invited to a fancy Italian gala and bring me as her plus one, and there I meet a handsome teenage count wearing a tuxedo who has longed to meet the English girl of his dreams and go on vacation to London."

"She's using me," I said, sticking my tongue out at her.

"You're of no use to me if you're not making the most of your fame advantage. Do you know how many free clothes she gets? Do you know how many she gives to me?"

"It's a little tricky considering you tower over me," I laughed, defending myself. "They send things in my size. You're too statuesque and model-like, I'm afraid."

"You're right," she sighed. "Most of them wouldn't cover my bottom."

James made me smile by laughing out loud.

"She got sent that little dress she's wearing, don't you know," Jess informed him, knowingly. "It was made just for her."

"Oh, er, yes. It looks like it was. Excellent dress, Anna."

"Okay, you're being weird." I laughed, but then looked up to see James looking oddly awkward.

Jess raised her eyebrows and looked at both of us

carefully. "Well, would you just look at that chili! I'll be back in a second, guys. I have to get a photo of the chili!" And off she ran.

She disappeared into the crowd, leaving James and I alone to stare at a box of absurdly large avocados.

13.

From: connorlawrence1@zingmail.co.uk
To: anna_huntley@zingmail.co.uk
Subject: Re: Congratulations!

Spidey, I'm so sorry it's taken me this long to reply to your messages—thanks so much for the congratulations e-mail and the voice mail you left me. Hearing your voice cheered my day! I really appreciate your support, especially as I can tell you that there is an agent officially interested in my work. Seriously! And she's asked to see more examples, but of course I don't really have anything.

So I am spending every minute of the day working on the second storyline of *The Amazing It Girl* and trying to come up with some random sketches to show her so she can see some variety in my work. Do you think that's a good idea? I wish you were here to give me some advice!

I told her on the phone that you inspired the Ember character and she said she'd love to meet you when you're back. Maybe you could come to one of the meetings with me? I know you'd probably be embarrassed about it, but I would feel so much better having you by my side.

How's Rome? You still having a good time? Have you tried the Nutella ice cream yet? Anyway, I better go—I need to work on my bad guy! At the moment, he looks like a cross between an old man and a llama. Not my scariest work . . .

Connor

xx

Wow, this is boring.

Jess! You can't pass notes in the middle of a lecture!

Why not? It's way more interesting than listening to this dude talk.

This DUDE happens to be one of Italy's most esteemed gallery owners. And I happen to find what he's saying very interesting.

Oh, really? What's he talking about, then?

What do you mean?

If you're listening so hard, what's he talking about?

Duh. Art.

What kind of art?

I'm not going to play your silly games.

Ha! You have no idea what he's talking about. Admit it.

I absolutely know what he's talking about. Something to do with paint.

Yeah, you really proved me wrong there.

As an artist yourself, you should at least be making notes.

I am making notes. And then passing them to you.

I'm not sure that counts.

Talking of art, have you heard back from Connor yet?

Yes! An agent is really interested in his stuff. Looks like he made the right decision to stay at home in the end!

Do you think so? I don't. We've had the BEST time. Although, he probably wouldn't have enjoyed it so much.

What do you mean?

You know, he's not that into organized fun, is he? He wouldn't have wanted to do any of the activities. He's

too shy for that kind of thing. Can you imagine Connor trying circus skills??

I think he'd look rather dashing on a tightrope.

Of course you do. Are you sure you want to miss out on the spaghetti-making this evening?

I'll see you guys after for ice cream. Uh-oh. I think Mrs. Ginnwell is looking this way. She doesn't look happy.

Nope. She's gesturing something. What is she trying to say?

Something not great by the looks of it. Why is she wriggling her hand around?

I think she's motioning a writing action.

And now she's doing a slitting-throat action.

That's never a good sign.

I think she's coming over.

She looks very angry.

We should probably stop writing notes before she catches us.

Lucky we're so stealthy about it.

We're like spies. Only we don't pass international secrets.

Wait. She just mouthed "stop passing notes."

I think she knows.

"I hear you're missing out on the spaghetti-making class to speak to your dad," Sophie announced as she swanned past my bed into the bathroom before emerging with a large travel bag. "Trouble in paradise?"

"No," I sighed, trying to focus on painting my toenails without smudging. "We're just having a chat. I'm not that concerned about spaghetti."

"You are such a bad liar," she said. "If you're going to lie, you can't distort your face like that. It gives the game away."

I didn't say anything in the hope she would drop it, but of course I was talking to Sophie Parker, who, in past experience, had never held back at the risk of hurting other people's feelings.

"Is it true what they're saying in the magazines, then?" she asked, sitting at the dressing table in front of the mirror and whipping out some mascara to reapply.

"I already told you that Tom and Marianne are—"

"Not about them. About your dad and Helena."

I froze, a dollop of nail polish dripping off the brush and onto the carpet. I rubbed it in with my toe. "What are the magazines saying?"

She stood up and walked over to her bed, throwing a batch of magazines across to me. I glanced down to see a picture of Helena and my dad on the front cover with a great big white zigzag running down the center of the magazine splitting the picture and loads of Italian words in bold red with exclamation points.

"I got the receptionist to translate it for me." She picked up her mascara again. "And, just to emphasize, I did *not* buy it because it had your weird family on the cover. Italian magazines have way better fashion pages."

"What does it say? It's usually all garbage."

"It says the wedding is *supposed* to be on the twenty-third of August."

"What?" I put the nail polish down and picked up the top magazine. "How did they find that out?"

"It says it's on the twenty-third of August and is being held at the Tilney Hotel in London." Sophie turned to watch my reaction. "Oh . . . so it's not *all* garbage, then?"

"What is the article saying?"

"I don't know." She snorted, turning back to her reflection. "Why would I waste my time asking the receptionist to translate the whole article about *your* family? Who cares anyway?"

I flicked to the main article, staring at all the pictures of Dad and Helena and the images of broken hearts dotted around them.

I don't know whether Sophie noticed my worried expression or if she liked the idea of being involved somehow, but, either way, she let out a sigh and came to sit down next to me on the bed.

"So the implication is they might break up. And the receptionist said something about too much fame—her English wasn't spot on so that doesn't make much sense, but here"—she pointed at one of the sentences with her long blue fingernail—"*pressione* means pressure, so we can guess . . . too much pressure. And here in this sentence it says *anormale*, which I imagine means abnormal. And it has your dad's name in the same sentence so maybe . . . it's abnormal for him. Or maybe your dad's just abnormal?" She smirked at her own joke.

She leaned back. "Don't scowl at me, Anna! I'm helping you. So, summing it up, I'd say the article is about your dad finding getting married to a big celebrity like Helena very stressful and it's giving him second thoughts." She rolled her eyes and stood up to go back to the dressing table. "Like that's news."

"You're not surprised by any of this?" I said, gesturing to the pile of magazines, all showing pictures of Helena looking concerned or upset in them.

"Duh," she said, applying her bright red lip gloss. "You are so naive it's embarrassing. It's a celebrity wedding, Anna, not a real one."

"That doesn't make any sense," I said, shaking my head.

"Yeah, it does. Everyone knows that when you're famous, relationships just aren't the same. You can't date a celebrity and have a normal life, and you certainly can't marry one and expect to have a normal wedding."

"You're wrong."

She sighed, swiveled on the stool to face me, crossed her long, slender legs, and leaned forward, clasping her hands together as though explaining a life lesson to a small child. "Anna, do you think Connor enjoys being photographed when he's out with you?"

"No, of course not, but—"

"Not that I know the freak all that well, but considering he has never once partaken in any school activity that requires socializing with normal people, I'm going to take a wild guess and say that being in the limelight is his idea of hell."

"He's not a fan, but that doesn't—"

"He's not mature enough for all that attention. Not that any of the boys in our year are very mature," she huffed, pursing her lips. "Brendan thinks it's cool to skim coins across the Trevi Fountain and splash my favorite dress at the same time. I bet Italian boys don't do stuff like that."

"Connor knew about the photographers before we started dating," I pointed out, not wanting to go off-topic, "but he still asked me out."

"Sure, he likes you and your dad likes Helena Montaine. Who wouldn't? Helena, that is. She's glamorous and beautiful," Sophie said, flicking back her hair. "But he's going to have to put up with a lifetime of reporters following his every move and printing his every mistake. Like I said"—she moved to pick up her handbag, throwing her lip gloss and mascara into it—"you can't have a normal relationship with a celebrity. Why do you think the paparazzi even *exists*? You can't report on boring, normal, happy relationships. The paps report on celebrity relationships, because they are none of those things."

"My dad is happy," I croaked, my head spinning at what she was saying.

"Anna, you're missing an evening of fun just to phone him," she said, raising her eyebrows. "I don't think you believe that."

I looked down at the magazines on the bed. Sophie shook her head and walked toward the door. She stopped as she reached for the handle and spun her head around to look at me, her glossy, highlighted hair swishing over her shoulders.

"It's the price of fame, right? Actors, models, singers, It Girls. They don't usually get a happy ending." She stood by the door watching me closely as I kept my head bowed, tracing the zigzag breaking up the photo of Helena and Dad on the magazine with my finger.

"Anna . . ." She hesitated and I thought I saw a look of genuine sympathy. She opened her mouth, about to say something, but then caught herself and pulled out her cell phone instead, distracted by a message. "I have a toe separator," she said hurriedly, not looking at me. "It will help you not to smudge the nail polish. It's in that travel bag if you want to borrow it."

She put her phone away, fished her sunglasses out of her bag, slid them onto the top of her head, and left the room.

If we hadn't been talking about something so worrying, it might just have been a nice moment.

I slammed the magazine down on the bed and reached for the phone, but it started ringing. "Hello?"

"Anna? Is that you?"

"Hey, Helena. Good timing—I was just about to call home!"

"Anna, I'm calling about Marianne."

"What?" I asked, suddenly processing her frenzied tone. "What is it? What's wrong?"

"Tom broke up with her." Helena paused, her breathing short and panicked. "She's gone missing."

14.

From: anna_huntley@zingmail.co.uk

To: rebecca.blythe@bounce-mail.co.uk;

helena@montaines.co.uk

Subject: Places where Marianne might be

1. Her bedroom

She may have boarded up the door with her
wardrobe or chest of drawers, like that time
I tried to get out of school because Dad was
ruining my life.

2. The broom closet

The first place you probably would go when
feeling upset, like that time when I lied to
Jess and the time before Sports Day and all
the other times that I have humiliated myself,
which has pretty much been every day since I
emerged from the womb.

3. The comic-book store

A very good place to go to when people are annoying you, like that time when Dad got all mad just because I threw a pork pie at his head and I had to get out of the house.

4. Walking around the park with Dog

Dog has a very calm aura and is an excellent listener. The only disadvantage is his attention span, like that time I was midway through telling him about how I was pretty sure I'd swallowed a spider the night before, but then he ran off to fetch me that dead mouse and made all the children near us cry.

Have you checked all these? Report back immediately.

Love, me xxx

From: rebecca.blythe@bounce-mail.co.uk
To: helena@montaines.co.uk;
anna_huntley@zingmail.co.uk
Subject: Re: Places where Marianne might be
Wonderful, Anna, thank you!

Quick question though, darling, are you aware that it's Marianne who is missing and not you?
Mom xxx

From: anna_huntley@zingmail.co.uk
To: rebecca.blythe@bounce-mail.co.uk;
helena@montaines.co.uk
Subject: Re: Places where Marianne might be
Yes, Mom, thank you. I am aware that I am not missing.
I'm just showing you the inner workings of a teenager's mind. Marianne probably thinks the same way I do.
Love, me xxx

From: rebecca.blythe@bounce-mail.co.uk
To: helena@montaines.co.uk;
anna_huntley@zingmail.co.uk
Subject: Re: Places where Marianne might be
Oh, I see! Well then, we will be sure to check all those spots.

If we're going along those lines, then we should also check the store cupboard of the local supermarket.

Anna once sneaked in there, Helena, when she was in a mood and I wasn't looking. She found their stock of Nutella and climbed in one of the boxes with all those jars.

The staff were really very lovely about the whole saga—as you can imagine I was in quite a state looking for her.

Very lucky that the kind man who worked behind the fish counter heard her talking to the jars in the box about her problems as she started eating from one, otherwise we might never have found her!

xxx

From: helena@montaines.co.uk
To: rebecca.blythe@bounce-mail.co.uk;
anna_huntley@zingmail.co.uk
Subject: Re: Places where Marianne might be

You know, Marianne is fond of marmalade!

I'll try the supermarket next to my house.

Helena x

From: rebecca.blythe@bounce-mail.co.uk
To: helena@montaines.co.uk;
anna_huntley@zingmail.co.uk
Subject: Re: Places where Marianne might be

I'll try the one next to Nick's house.

Rebecca xxx

From: anna_huntley@zingmail.co.uk
To: rebecca.blythe@bounce-mail.co.uk;
helena@montaines.co.uk
Subject: Re: Places where Marianne might be

And I'll try to pretend that Mom never told that story to anyone ever.

From: rebecca.blythe@bounce-mail.co.uk
To: helena@montaines.co.uk;
anna_huntley@zingmail.co.uk
Subject: Re: Places where Marianne might be

Let's be optimistic and keep our spirits up

working as a team!

Thunderbirds are away!

Rebecca x

From: helena@montaines.co.uk
To: rebecca.blythe@bounce-mail.co.uk;
anna_huntley@zingmail.co.uk
Subject: Re: Places where Marianne might be

Wonderful, Rebecca! You really are the best help I could ever have asked for.

Although, I think you got that line slightly wrong. I believe it is . . .

Thunderbirds are up and away!

Helena x

From: rebecca.blythe@bounce-mail.co.uk
To: helena@montaines.co.uk;
anna_huntley@zingmail.co.uk
Subject: Re: Places where Marianne might be

Oh, of course, how silly of me! I always get these wrong, don't I, Anna? How infuriating for you.

Thunderbirds are up and away!

Rebecca x

From: anna_huntley@zingmail.co.uk

To: rebecca.blythe@bounce-mail.co.uk;

helena@montaines.co.uk

Subject: Re: Places where Marianne might be

THUNDERBIRDS ARE GO! It is one of the most famous lines of all time!!!!

HOW DID YOU NOT GET THAT RIGHT?!

I'm going to go put a cold compress on my head.

Love, me xxx

"Anna, I need you to be focused right now," Danny demanded, looking perplexed as I came to sit down with my Nutella ice cream.

"Relax, Danny, she can eat ice cream and answer your questions at the same time," Jess pointed out. "She hasn't spent the last hour gorging herself on spaghetti like we have."

"Yeah, Danny," I said in a very serious tone. "I am one hundred percent focused on the matter in hand."

I took a bite of my ice cream.

Five times in my life that I've eaten something and it has taken me by surprise:

1. When I ate a mussel because the sauce they were in smelled really good and then it was so gross I spat it out and it landed in this woman's hair and we had to leave the restaurant.

2. When I tried a curry that I thought was mild, but it was spicy, so I reached for Dad's drink, the nearest to me, and I poured the whole glass into my mouth without realizing it was wine and then I spat it out all over the table and we had to leave the restaurant.

3. When I tried lobster and it was disgusting but I felt bad as it was expensive, so I picked it up and made it do a funny dance to entertain Dad, but one of its pincers flew off during a high kick and it hit a man in the head and we had to leave the restaurant.

4. When I ate some black pudding and then Dad told me what it was and I was sick on the floor and we had to leave the restaurant.

5. When I tried the gelato in this ice-cream parlor in Rome and thought that my head was about to explode it was so good and then made

the quick yet wise decision that I would have to
move to Italy and forge a career in ice cream
just so I could be near it.

"Wow, you wolfed that down pretty fast," Jess observed,
looking impressed as I started on my second scoop.

"Seriously, what do they put in this ice cream?" I asked,
holding up the carton in wonder. "You guys all have to try
some."

"Yes, please!" Stephanie said, happily taking the spoon I
passed her.

"Focus, please!" Danny repeated, rapping his knuckles on
the table. "Anna, where do you think Marianne might be?
Think."

I took a deep breath and buried my head in my hands, eyes
shut tightly to concentrate as much as possible.

"She could be anywhere," Jess said, taking the spoon
from Stephanie for her turn. "It's not like she doesn't have the
means to just jump on a plane somewhere last minute."

"I wish she'd just turn her phone on. Helena told me it's
been switched off this whole time," I mumbled.

"Don't worry, Anna. She'll probably just be trying to get

away from the press, and him, too," Stephanie soothed. "She'll get in touch soon enough."

"So when was she last seen?" Danny asked.

"Helena said she was with her in their house when she got the text from Tom—"

"He did it by text?" Jess asked, her eyes widening. "Scoundrel!"

"What else did Helena say?" Danny persisted.

"Marianne ran upstairs and that was it," I shrugged. "The door was shut. Helena came downstairs to call your dad, and by the time she was off the phone, Marianne's room was empty."

"Tom's house!" Danny asked, his eyes lighting up. "She'll have gone there! Perhaps to try and win him back?"

"He's on tour," I reminded him.

"It's all over the Internet already," Stephanie said, biting her lip. "It's the main headline on most of the big sites."

"What do they say? How do they even know?" I groaned, dropping my head back into my hands, wishing this wasn't happening.

"Well." Stephanie gulped. "There are these rumors."

"What rumors?" I looked up.

"That he's met someone else," she said hurriedly. "But they're just rumors."

"He's meant to be moving in with her," I said, completely aghast. "He can't have met someone else."

"None of that matters right now," Danny announced in a sensible manner. "It's probably just lies. You know the way it is."

"Danny's right," Jess said. "Probably a load of garbage."

"They were right about the wedding details," I said.

James suddenly appeared by our booth holding a magazine. He slid in next to Jess, who offered him the spoon for some ice cream.

"Hey," he said, "any luck on finding Marianne?"

"Not yet," Stephanie sighed. "She's still missing."

"I think there's something we can do," he said, slapping the magazine down on the table in front of us.

"What am I looking at?"

"Tom Kyzer is on tour. Guess where he's playing tomorrow night?" We all blinked back at him, clueless. "*Rome*. He's playing here in Rome."

"Are you serious?" Everyone leaned forward to look closer at the magazine as I desperately smoothed out the glossy pages to have a proper look. "This is all in Italian."

"You can get the idea," he said with a shrug. "I checked it against his website to be sure. It's certain. He's playing at this giant venue called Atlantico. Bob Dylan once played there."

Danny, who had been peering at the magazine curiously, pulled away. "You think Marianne has come here to Rome?"

"Maybe!" James shrugged. "Or if not, then Tom might have an idea where she could be."

"James!" I gasped. "You're a genius! He must be able to tell me something."

"Right! How are we going to sneak out and get there?" Jess asked, excitedly.

"Hang on." My eyes scanned their faces. "You guys can't come with me."

"Why not?" Jess said indignantly, hands on hips.

"If we're caught, you'll get into big trouble," I pointed out. "Plus it's going to be really difficult to do—we'll have to somehow sneak out of the hotel tomorrow night and then sneak back in."

"We can do that," Danny said, lifting his chin defiantly. "It's not like we haven't snuck into places before."

"Look, I really don't think—"

"Anna, shush," Jess interrupted, laughing. "You're never going to get away with the whole scheme without us. Have you met you?"

"You're not doing this on your own," James added firmly. "We're in, whether you like it or not."

Danny and Stephanie both nodded vigorously before holding hands and beaming at each other.

"You two are gross, by the way," Jess observed.

"Tomorrow night, then." I took a deep breath. "All we need to do is worm our way into one of the biggest music venues in Rome and talk to a rock star who has dumped my future step-sister over text." I bit my lip nervously. "And, weirdly, the bit I'm most scared about? Trying to get out of the hotel without Mrs. Ginnwell noticing."

"Sneaking away from teachers?" James grinned at me. "It's a piece of cake."

15.

"LET ME GET THIS STRAIGHT," CONNOR SAID, ONCE I'd finally managed to get through to him on the phone. "You're all planning on sneaking out, strolling into a massive music venue, and asking Tom Kyzer if he can help you track down the girl he has just broken up with."

"Yes."

"And . . . did you just say Brendan Dakers is helping?"

"That is correct. He's a recent addition."

There was a pause. "Are you *serious*?"

"Yes!" I sighed, anxious for him to agree it was a good idea and not fuel the worries I'd already had myself. "I know it sounds crazy but—"

"Just a bit. Anna, how are you even planning on getting backstage? There will be bouncers."

"James reckons that they'll recognize me. It's plausible—I

have been in the papers here a lot the past few days. I'll just tell them that Tom is expecting me."

"I'm not sure about this."

I ran a hand through my hair. I was nervous enough as it was and I didn't have long until the plan had to kick into gear.

"How's the drawing?" I asked, deciding to change the subject.

"It's going well . . . ," he said, sounding a bit brighter. "I can't wait for you to see what I've done. I've really gone for it with some of the characters. Of course," he added softly, "I would have loved your input. You're brilliant at that sort of thing."

"Don't be silly." I smiled at the phone. "I'm not creative at all. You're the one with all the talent."

"I do wish you were back here, Anna."

I beamed.

"But I'm really sorry. I have to go now," he said. I gripped the receiver, not wanting our conversation to be over quite yet. I needed to feel comforted and my stomach was still doing somersaults. "I've got loads to finish tonight."

"Okay," I said, swallowing my disappointment. "No

worries. I'm really looking forward to seeing all your new characters. They sound amazing."

"Listen, don't do anything rash. I know what show-offs James and Brendan can be. I don't want you getting in trouble because of some stupid idea they had—especially that joker Brendan. I'm worried because I care."

"I know."

And I did know. After we'd hung up, I thought about how Connor had always been there for me when everyone else was either trying to be my friend because of my newly found fame or just plain laughing at the ridiculous situations my famous self had gotten into. Like hanging upside down in a waterfall—or singing to a hall of people who really didn't want to hear me sing. I wondered if this were another of those situations? If I should even be going ahead with it.

Connor's worry about Brendan was a fair one. James had had to convince a VERY skeptical audience the next morning that his involvement was a good idea.

We'd all been sitting on the Spanish Steps while Miss Lawler got ready to tell us about the official plans for the day.

"What a wonderful moment, eh, boys and girls?" she asked, looking up from her clipboard and interrupting our in-depth discussion about what I should say to Tom Kyzer.

"Just be quiet for one second and look around you. It's not about the steps themselves—it's about the atmosphere, the people around you, the beautiful fountain at the bottom of these steps, the Trinità dei Monti Church at the top, the sun shining, the blue skies, being with your friends." She inhaled deeply. "There won't be many moments in life as glorious as this one. Take it all in."

My eyes scanned all the people bustling around us, sitting in groups and chattering over the sound of the splashing, trickling water from the fountain. I closed my eyes and felt the sun on my face.

"Anna is really taking it all in." I heard Jess snicker.

"Shut up." I smiled without opening my eyes, leaning my head on her shoulder. She leaned hers on top of mine. Jess was right about Connor missing out, I thought. There's no way I would want to have missed this.

That was when James leaned in and dropped the bombshell about Brendan's role in that evening's sneaking-away-from-the-teachers plan.

"But how do we know that he won't snitch on us? Are we sure he's up to it?" Jess asked, searching the mass of heads in front of us and spotting Brendan hitting one of his friends with his flip-flop before bursting out laughing as though it was the funniest thing he'd ever done.

"He's the best at stuff like this," James insisted.

"Breaking the rules?" Stephanie asked.

"Exactly."

"Are you sure? I don't remember Brendan ever being in trouble," I said, thinking of all those times I was in detention last year. It had just been me and Connor.

"That's because he's never been caught," James replied coolly.

"What's his plan?" I asked, now watching Brendan wave his flip-flop in Sophie's face, who was going, "Ewwww, Brendan, gross! Go annoy someone else!"

"No idea," James chuckled. "But I have no doubt he'll think of something that will get us safely out of the vicinity without Mrs. Ginnwell suspecting a thing."

"I hope you're right about this, James," Jess said.

"I am," he said firmly. "You're all just going to have to trust me."

Hi, you have reached Nick Huntley's phone. Please leave your name, number, and any message and I'll get back to you as soon as possible. Thank you.

BEEP

"Hi, Nick, it's Rebecca! You remember me, the mother of your only child? I remind you only because you haven't replied to any of my messages. Why aren't you answering your phone? Can't you hear the phone ringing anymore? It wouldn't surprise me at all considering your age. Would you like me to ask my friend Colin about hearing aids? He's been wearing one a few years now so I'm sure he can recommend a good set. If, however, you're heading down the route of 'selective hearing' and CHOOSING not to pick up the phone, I'll be very angry indeed, Nicholas. I expect that sort of thing from Dog, not you. I'll call back in a minute once I've spoken to Colin and I hope you will have grown up in the meantime."

Hi, you have reached Nick Huntley's phone. Please leave your name, number, and any message and I'll get back to you as soon as possible. Thank you.

BEEP

"Hello, darling, it's me, Helena. I've been thinking, do you think Marianne could be at the aquarium? She has always been fond of penguins. I'll give them a call now to check and let you know what they say."

Hi, you have reached Nick Huntley's phone. Please leave your name, number, and any message and I'll get back to you as soon as possible. Thank you.

  BEEP

  "Nick, it's Rebecca again. Do you know, I was so distracted by your childish behavior or possible lack of hearing that I completely forgot to tell you why I was calling in the first place! I was going to ask you whether you think Marianne could be at Stonehenge. I remember her once saying she was interested in old architecture and that's just about the oldest architecture I can think of. I'm about to give my friend Stanley a call. He lives near Wiltshire so I'll ask him if he can drive over and check. I'll let you know what he says."

Hi, you have reached Nick Huntley's phone. Please leave your name, number, and any message and I'll get back to you as soon as possible. Thank you.

  BEEP

  "Hi, darling, it's me again. The man at the aquarium was VERY rude just now. When I asked him if he had seen Marianne Montaine lurking anywhere in the vicinity, he told me he had no time for prank callers, especially when he was in the middle of a cuttlefish emergency, and then hung up! I intend to file a formal complaint! I will call them back and ask for the name of the manager and don't try and stop me. I will let you know what they say."

Hi, you have reached Nick Huntley's phone. Please leave your name, number, and any message and I'll get back to you as soon as possible. Thank you.

    BEEP

    "Nick, it's Rebecca again. Stanley is not picking up his phone. I had better get on the phone to Colin immediately. Looks like quite a few of my acquaintances need hearing aids. . . ."

Hi, you have reached Nick Huntley's phone. Please leave your name, number, and any message and I'll get back to you as soon as possible. Thank you.

    BEEP

    "You'll never believe what the aquarium has done now. When I phoned them to say that I, Helena Montaine, was most displeased with one of their staff members and could I have the name of their manager, the man on the end of the phone laughed and then said that the manager's name was Mr. Not-an-idiot and then he hung up AGAIN. I hope you're going to do something about this, Nicholas—for example, write a very bad review of that aquarium in one of the magazines you work for. That will show them!"

Hi, you have reached Nick Huntley's phone. Please leave your name, number, and any message and I'll get back to you as soon as possible. Thank you.

BEEP

"Hey, Dad, it's me. Why aren't you picking up your phone? You know, I have been thinking recently you may be a bit deaf these days, but I didn't say anything because I know you're sensitive about being old and everything. Jess has let me borrow her phone to tell you that we're going to go speak to Tom Kyzer because he's here in Rome! You never know, Marianne might be hiding around here somewhere. Anyway, I better go because I'm on a fire escape and need both hands to climb down the next bit. Bye!"

From: nicholas.huntley@bounce-mail.co.uk
To: helena@montaines.co.uk;
Cc: anna_huntley@zingmail.co.uk;
rebecca.blythe@bounce-mail.co.uk;
Subject: Voice mails

Well, this has made my day.

Rebecca—NO, I do not think that Marianne is hiding behind one of the pillars of Stonehenge. I can only imagine that your head got pecked so many times during the six months you spent in South Africa looking after ostriches that you are getting confused with what is normal and what is not.

Helena—leave the poor aquarium people alone. Didn't you hear the man? He has a cuttlefish emergency on his hands!

Anna—I don't even want to *know* why you're on a fire escape at the moment. Get. Down.

I imagine that what Marianne really needs is her space, so all three of you need to stop this ridiculous plotting and let her come to us when she's ready.

Do you know what I was just thinking? Dog is the only member of my family who hasn't lost their mind today.

And considering he ate a fork earlier, I think that says a lot about all of you.

Nicholas/Dad x

PS I am now going to pour myself a large whiskey and won't be picking up the phone for the rest of the day. Blame that on my hearing if you wish. It is nice to have an excuse.

16.

THE FIRE ESCAPE WAS ALL PART OF BRENDAN'S self-titled Genius Plan.

"I used it the other day," he mentioned casually when we were all gathered in my room to hear how he planned on getting us out. "You can just climb right on down."

"Why can't we just quietly sneak out the front door?" Jess asked.

"Too risky. The teachers sit in the lounge reading and doing other boring stuff and they have a perfect view of the reception area. Plus I know for a fact that the hotel staff have been instructed to inform teachers if they see any students leave the building and to question said students before they go out." He shrugged. "I guess they're used to people trying to sneak out on school trips."

"How do you know all this?" Stephanie asked him, her eyes peeking out below her bangs, wide with awe.

"I was chatting to the lady behind the reception desk," he grinned. "I asked her out for a slice of pizza."

"Oh yeah?" James laughed. "How well did that go down?"

"She had already eaten."

"Sure." Jess rolled her eyes.

I was going to ask why he would do that when he's meant to be dating Sophie, but I didn't want to annoy him while he was doing me a favor. Plus Sophie didn't seem like she was all that enamored with him these days.

"I still don't understand why you want to help us," said Jess.

"For the same reason James does . . ." Brendan shrugged. James snapped his head up looking at Brendan intently as everyone else waited for James to explain.

"It's fun to break the rules," Brendan finished, laughing and answering for him.

I sighed, feeling strangely disappointed without knowing quite why. Maybe Connor had been right about the pair of them.

"Okay, so we just go down the fire escape. Easy." Danny nodded.

"Slight snag is the big window in the lounge." Brendan explained. "The fire escape goes right past it and if anyone sees the lot of you climbing down outside, game over. That's where I come in."

"What's your plan?" I asked.

The plan, Brendan informed us, was simple and yet effective, requiring minimal effort but maximum results:

1. Brendan sneaks us to the fire escape without anyone seeing
2. We climb down the fire escape.
3. We stop before the lounge window.
4. Brendan and Sophie stage a huge, explosive fight in the reception area—

"Wait a minute!" I interrupted. "What was that last point?"

"Myself and Sophie stage a huge fight in the reception area and then—"

"Sophie?" Jess gaped. "There is no way you are getting *Sophie* involved in this."

"I need her to help." Brendan shrugged. "It's realistic that I get in a fight with Sophie."

"I reckon that makes sense." James nodded.

"No way!" Jess shrieked. "Brendan was one thing—no offense, Brendan," she added, but he didn't look too bothered. "But Sophie Parker? We can't trust Sophie Parker. She HATES us. She will tell everyone! She'd love to see us get in trouble! Plus you'll never get her to agree. She said categorically at the beginning of the trip that she would never want to be on the same team as us."

"Jess might be right," Danny said, his forehead furrowed in concern. "We shouldn't get Sophie involved in this."

"Oh, please," came a snide voice as my bedroom door swung open and Sophie strode in, slamming and locking it behind her. "I already know about the whole thing. Oh, and by the way, you should keep your voices down. It's lucky no one is listening in the corridor."

She came to stand next to Brendan, victoriously observing all our shocked faces.

"Stop freaking out," Sophie sighed, rearranging her mini skirt and smoothing her hair. "I'm happy to help."

"*You* are happy to help *us*?" I asked.

"Yes," she replied, beginning to look bored by the situation already. "But if I'm going to help you sneak out, then I want something in return."

"This is REALLY not good," Jess cried, burying her head in her hands.

"What?" I asked dubiously.

"An invite." She focused her eyes determinedly on me. "To the wedding. Your dad's wedding."

"*What?*"

She reached for her lip gloss and began to apply it as she spoke. "I want an invite to your dad's wedding. Don't worry about the ceremony. But I want to be at the reception. The big party. That is, *if* the wedding still takes place, which according to the *Daily Post* is pretty unlikely," she added.

"I can't get you an invite to their *wedding*? Are you CRAZY?"

She popped the lid back on her lip gloss. "If you want my help, I'm going to have to insist on it."

I ran my fingers through my hair, glancing at Jess, who was shaking her head in disbelief. James, admittedly, also looked pained at the situation. "I can *try* to get you into the reception. I don't know why you of all people would want to go to my dad's wedding."

"It's the most exclusive event of the year. I heard that Leonardo DiCaprio is invited. I want to be there." She said. "Duh. So, do we have a deal?"

Brendan grinned. "We really can't do it without her."

I looked at James, who shrugged.

I sighed. "Yeah. We have a deal."

"Now that we've got that sorted," Brendan continued as Sophie smiled smugly, "I will continue with my plan."

1. Brendan sneaks us to the fire escape without anyone seeing.

2. We climb down the fire escape.

3. We stop before the lounge window.

4. Brendan and Sophie stage a huge, explosive fight in the reception area.

5. The teachers intervene.

6. We quickly make our way past the window and safely on to the road.

7. Brendan and Sophie wait until we're no longer visible before staging a makeup.

8. The teachers go back to their reading.

9. Brendan is hailed as king of the world.

10. ("More like king of the doofuses" in Jess's opinion.)

"And you guys go talk to Tom Kyzer, who will hopefully have his shirt off at the time," Sophie concluded, distracted by moisturizing her new tan lines. "Don't worry about it—it's a foolproof plan."

"I never thought I'd say this," Jess sighed, lying back across the bed and covering her face in her hands, "but I really hope Sophie is right."

* * *

Later that evening, we sat huddled on the steel-grated platform of the fire escape from which a set of steps spiraled down to the ground.

"Is it safe?" Stephanie asked anxiously. "It doesn't feel very stable."

"It should hold. Granted there was only one of me and there's five of you, but, hey, let's see what happens. . . . Right," Brendan whispered, rubbing his hands together as Stephanie peered down the steps, and Danny moved protectively in front of her, "it's showtime. I'll go get Sophie. You guys should be able to hear us through the window, but you'll definitely be able to see the teachers get up to sort us out if you angle yourself on the steps right. Just make sure you don't get seen."

Brendan gave us a thumbs-up, high-fived James, and then slammed the fire exit shut.

"No going back now." I gulped.

"Come on, then." James grinned, ruffling my hair and making his way down the steps. We all followed, gripping onto the cold, steel rail and hurrying down the side of the hotel in a single-file line. James stopped just as we stood above the lounge window and held up his hand to bring us all to a halt.

"I can see Mr. Kenton reading his book. Brendan should

be there any minute now," he whispered. I was standing so close to James that my chin was almost touching his back, while Jess was leaning forward behind me with both her hands on my shoulders, gripping them nervously.

Suddenly we heard a loud crash, making Stephanie gasp and my breath catch in my throat. There was an explosion of shouting and I heard the shrill shriek of Sophie's voice piercing through the bustle of stern, raised voices.

"Go! Go! Go!" James signaled, rushing down the steps. We hurried down and soon enough we were all past the window, onto the street, and around the corner out of sight.

"What was that bang?" Jess asked, as she unzipped my backpack and got out the map.

"They must have broken something for added effect," James chuckled.

"Annoyingly, Sophie played that very well," Jess muttered. She turned to me with a sympathetic smile. "I don't know how you're going to explain to Helena that you're bringing your school enemy as a date to her wedding."

I grimaced, wondering whether I could persuade Sophie to sneak into the wedding via a back entrance the same way we were doing tonight. I doubted it.

"Right, this way," Danny instructed, shoving the map in

his pocket and helpfully distracting me. "We need to hurry if we're going to make it before the concert starts."

We set off down the cobbled streets in the evening warmth, none of us really saying much because if the others were feeling anything like I was then we were all concentrating on controlling our nerves. I hadn't really planned what I was going to say when I got there; I was sort of hoping that I might just see Marianne wandering around and be able to pounce on her.

"You okay?" James asked as we eventually approached the stadium. "You look pale."

"It's just . . . I never normally do stuff like this." I confessed, swallowing the lump in my throat. "It's a bit out of character for me."

"Really?" James looked surprised. "I don't think so."

It was my turn to look surprised.

"Being there for your friends and family in their times of need? That sounds very much like you," he explained simply.

"I was talking about deliberately breaking the rules."

"Yeah, well, maybe it's a new side to your character." He smiled. "No one stays the same forever. I think it suits you."

"Hey, rule breaker," Jess said gently, nudging me for

attention. "It looks like Tom Kyzer has a big fan base here in Italy." She nodded in the direction of the long line of On the Rox supporters ahead of us, many of them wearing T-shirts with Tom's face emblazoned across the front.

"That looks like the stage door. You see it?" James gestured toward a thin door at the side of the building where a large man was standing in black clothing with a radio in his ear. He was talking to a teenage boy with headphones around his neck, who I presumed must have been one of the sound guys.

"That bouncer looks like he should be in the army," Stephanie noted, taking in his height and muscles. "Do you really think this plan to get us in will work, James?" She bit her lip.

"Yes," James replied. "Jess, you have your camera, right?"

"As instructed." She grinned.

"And, Anna, you have your big sunglasses?"

"The biggest pair I own," I said, handing my backpack to Jess and putting them on.

"Perfect, you look like the It Girl you are," James said, clapping his hands together. "Everyone ready to put those acting skills to use? Jess, you're going to have to step it up and do even better than your best friend, Sophie. Her performance sounded pretty good back there."

"Please," she snorted, getting her camera ready. "I ALWAYS do better than Sophie."

James winked at me, whispered, "Anna, time to start walking. Channel your inner Marianne," and then gave Stephanie a sharp nod.

Having received her signal, she opened her mouth and screamed so loudly that all the On the Rox fans whipped their heads around to look our way. "IT'S ANNA HUNTLEY!!" she cried, grabbing Danny's arm and jumping up and down wildly. "IT'S ANNA HUNTLEY! TOM KYZER'S FRIEND!"

Danny and James leaped into role, shouting and cheering along with Stephanie, asking me questions and begging for a photo. Jess held up her camera and started skipping around me as I walked, the flash going off every second.

"Does anyone have a pen? I want her autograph!" Danny yelled toward the crowd of fans.

Instantly, the On the Rox fans broke rank and ran over.

I tried very hard not to (a) fall over or (b) feel intimidated as a huge group of screaming boys and girls sped toward us, pens and phones held out.

With the Rox fans having formed an excited mob around me, James, Danny, and Stephanie closed in protectively, now switching roles and acting as my exclusive and official entourage. I played my part, keeping my head down to get to the door, but occasionally looking up to smile and wave at them just like Marianne always does. The commotion was enough to get the bouncer's and the sound guy's attention, and they watched with interest as the crowd of chaos approached them.

"Excuse me," James said to the doorman. "Anna and her 'people' would like to come through."

The doorman looked suspiciously at James, holding up his hand firmly, but the crowd was getting more and more manic as stragglers on the road now joined to see if it was someone in the band, and the door got blocked.

"Please." I leaned in. "I'm Anna Huntley. I know Tom Kyzer, as I'm sure you're aware. I was hoping to sneak in without getting noticed." I smiled apologetically at the crowd. "Guess I should have known that die-hard fans of Tom Kyzer would recognize his friend!"

The bouncer said something in Italian into a microphone clipped to his jacket, held his finger to his ear as something came through his radio, and then nodded. He opened the door and the sound guy ushered us in.

The door slammed shut behind us. I heard James breathe a sigh of relief.

"You want Mr. Kyzer dressing room?" the sound guy asked with a strong Italian accent.

"If you would be so kind." Jess smiled, batting her eyelashes at him and running her eyes, not so subtly I might add, across his tanned, chiseled face and long dark hair. I saw Danny roll his eyes as the sound guy beamed back at her and led us down the corridor, asking her a load of questions as we confidently followed him.

After passing several security men and women dressed in black lined up along the corridor and greeting some of the stage managers, who stopped to shake my hand and tell me they were fans of the Iron Man incident, we were brought to a halt in front of a large purple door.

"Here," the sound guy said, before turning to Jess and holding out a small card for her to take. "My details." He passed it to her and she practically melted into the floor. "Give me a call. I take you for espresso."

As he walked down the corridor with a wave back at Jess, she grabbed my arm and squealed. "FINALLY!" She gave a big, dreamy sigh. "Thanks, Anna. I knew you'd come in useful one day."

Danny huffed. "Come on. We've got a job to do."

"Are you ready?" James asked, a reassuring hand on my

shoulder. I looked at the others who nodded back at me encouragingly. I took a deep breath and lifted my hand to the door.

But before I got the chance to knock, the door swung open and there was Tom Kyzer, holding hands with a girl who was gazing at him adoringly, ready to walk out by his side.

And it wasn't Marianne.

17.

THE THOUGHTS THAT WENT THROUGH MY BRAIN IN very quick succession when I saw Tom Kyzer standing in his dressing room holding hands with another girl when he'd only broken up with Marianne the day before, by text, were as follows:

1. WHAT?! No. NO!
2. Who is that girl? I have never seen her before!
3. No, wait, I have seen her before. Where have I seen her before?
4. That's it! The cover of *Vogue*. I've seen her on a cover of *Vogue*.
5. I remember seeing her on the cover of *Vogue* because she reminded me of a hammerhead shark.

6. You know the sharks with the eyes that are really spaced out?

7. That's what she reminded me of. A hammerhead shark.

8. A pretty hammerhead shark, granted. But a hammerhead shark, nonetheless.

9. How DARE Tom Kyzer dump Marianne for a hammerhead shark?!

10. IS HE CRAZY? I hate him.

11. I wish I knew how to do a karate chop.

12. Then I could karate chop him right now.

13. Although that might be hard to angle correctly.

14. I'd have to move around to karate chop his back.

15. I wish I could do a high kick.

16. Then I could high kick him in the face right now.

17. MAYBE I WILL HIGH KICK HIM IN THE FACE RIGHT NOW.

18. I might look stupid and injure myself.

19. I will not high kick him.

20. BUT I WILL STARE AT HIM IN ANGER.

Tom Kyzer looked as surprised to see me as I did to see Hammerhead-Shark Model holding his hand.

"*Anna?*"He gaped, immediately dropping her hand like it was on fire. "What are you doing here?"

Uh.

Think of something to say, Anna. You've dragged your friends all this way; they've risked getting in trouble for you. Say something intelligent and serious that will make Tom Kyzer realize the error of his ways.

"The sound guy took us down the corridor."

THE SOUND GUY TOOK US DOWN THE CORRIDOR?!

THAT'S THE BEST THING YOU COULD THINK TO SAY IN THAT MOMENT?!

Seriously, why am I on this planet? WHY?

He stared at me and I tried to form a sentence, but I just couldn't. My brain was going crazy trying to make sense of the situation we now were in.

All I could think of was the hurt that this stupid rock star had caused Marianne and how none of us even knew where she was right now and here he was acting as though he didn't care one jot about her.

"Anna has something to say," James announced, breaking

the silence before placing his hand gently on the small of my back. "Anna, come on. You are here for a reason."

I looked up at James and remembered all those times last semester that he said I could win the Sports Day trophy, even though I never believed I could.

"Tom," I began, taking a deep breath as James stepped back. "I need to know where Marianne is and whether you've heard from her. She's missing and I think you owe it to us to at least give us that information after the awful way you have treated her."

I thought that, considering my polite tone and reasonable query, he would at least look embarrassed or maybe even a little sad at the way things had turned out. But instead he started laughing.

Like the whole thing was *funny*.

I glanced at the others and was comforted to see they all looked baffled too.

"Anna." Tom shook his head. "Are you telling me you came all this way to ask me where Marianne is? I have no idea!" He glanced at Hammerhead-Shark Model standing behind him, who was looking at me curiously. "I seriously have no idea. Why would you even think I would know?"

"Why would I think you know? Because up until yesterday

you were her boyfriend and then you broke her heart and now she's missing. We're in Rome on a school trip and I thought she might come find you," I explained, my cheeks growing hot with anger.

"Well, she hasn't and, frankly, it would be weird if she did." He folded his arms and shifted his weight onto his back foot as if to emphasize how little he cared. "Marianne knows how this whole thing works. She knew what she was getting herself into."

"Trust me, she had no idea she was dating such a jerk." My anger at him had by now obliterated any feeling of shyness or embarrassment. It was bubbling away, ready to boil over. "You told her you wanted to move in with her!"

"Whoa, whoa," he said, lifting up his hands and once again glancing at Hammerhead-Shark Model, whose eyes were getting more and more narrow as the conversation proceeded, making her look even MORE like a hammerhead shark.

"She may have *mentioned* something along those lines"— Tom shrugged—"but it wasn't, you know, *serious*."

"How can you not see moving in together as serious?" I yelled.

One of the security men in the corridor coughed, reminding me of their presence, and I attempted to control the tone and pitch of my voice.

"I'm very confused, Tom. You were both in love. And then you just dropped her. How can that happen?"

"Look, Anna, it's just the world we live in. *You* know that!" He leaned toward me and gave me a playful punch on the arm, causing James to straighten up very quickly and Tom to immediately take a step back, recognizing that he probably shouldn't do that again.

"As I was saying, it's the world we live in," Tom continued, eyeing James nervously. "I'm a musician and Marianne is . . . well . . . an 'It Girl' or whatever you want to call it. We're both mixing in the same busy circles and things move on and they move fast. I'm on tour, meeting new people, gaining new experiences, finding myself through my music—"

Jess snorted loudly. Tom stopped abruptly and blinked at her before continuing.

"As I was saying, I'm finding myself through my music; Marianne has her, er, projects. I never saw it going anywhere."

"You should have told her that," I whispered, my eyes

prickling with tears. I couldn't believe that he had strung Marianne along all this time and made her think he felt the same way.

"Hey, Anna, look. We had fun, really we did," he said. "Like going to your Sports Day and hanging out all the time in London. We had some good times. But we're different."

"Different?" Stephanie piped up, looking utterly repulsed by him.

"Yeah, different," he said defensively, as though frustrated that he had to spell it out. "We're in the public eye. It's just an act. Everyone knows it wasn't a proper"—he searched for the word—"thing."

"You really have a way with words. That going to be a lyric in your next song?" Jess asked, folding her arms all sassily.

"Look, I think we're done here. But hey," Tom looked like he was going to nudge me on the shoulder again but then seemed to think better of it when James cleared his throat in warning. "No hard feelings, yeah?"

He smiled insincerely at me and reached back to hold out his hand to Hammerhead-Shark Model.

I can't pinpoint the exact reason I did what I did next.

Maybe it was the way he said "no hard feelings" so

casually and the way he had acted throughout our entire exchange.

Maybe it was the way he held out his hand to Hammerhead-Shark Model, as though he had the right to treat people the way he had treated Marianne and drop them without apology or responsibility.

Maybe it was the fact that, as he finished our conversation, a flash of Marianne's excited smile when she told us about Tom moving in with her crossed my mind.

Maybe it was for all these reasons that I just saw red.

Tom looked back to see why Hammerhead-Shark Model wasn't holding his hand, Jess shook her head in disgust, James looked as though he might punch Tom in the face any moment, and I just reached over toward the large jug of water that was on the shelf of his dressing room, lifted it high up in the air, and threw the water with as much strength as I could muster all over Tom Kyzer's stupid, pea-brain head.

A ripple of gasps filled the dressing room.

Tom Kyzer stood there, his sopping hair that had been expertly styled now stuck flat across his face and his black performance eyeliner trickling down his cheeks. His leather tasseled jacket and his T-shirt were soaked through, clinging to his body, and a puddle of water was forming around his drenched designer shoes.

Then the following happened:

1. James burst into the loudest laughter I have ever heard.

2. Jess and Danny followed suit.

3. Stephanie began applauding.

4. Tom Kyzer wiped the water out of his eyes and yelled, "WHAT THE HELL!"

5. Security ran into the room and saw Tom Kyzer drenched from head to foot.

6. One of them snickered, but covered it up before Tom saw.

7. Tom screamed, "GET THEM OUT!"

8. The five of us were grabbed by the arms and escorted out of the room.

9. As I was pulled into the corridor, Hammerhead-Shark Model whooped and shouted, "Girl Power!"

10. We all got thrown out of the building and back onto the street.

It turns out that our cunning plan to get into the building by causing a fuss around me had immediately gotten onto social media, so there were already hundreds of Italian reporters lurking around the stage door, hoping to get a new story on the latest Montaine drama.

They certainly got what they wanted.

Security didn't exactly throw us onto the ground, but they didn't graciously wave us good-bye either. Flashes started going off as soon as the stage door was opened and we were pushed unceremoniously back outside.

It can't have been that difficult for the Italian journalists to work out what was going on and it seemed they had brushed up on their English as they bombarded me with a hundred questions: "Anna, Anna, why were you thrown out?"; "Is this to do with Marianne's breakup?"; "Anna, is it true Tom is already dating supermodel Natalia?"; "Anna, is it true the wedding has been canceled?"; "Anna, were you thrown out for attacking Tom?"; "Anna, were you getting revenge?"; "Anna, is it true you held Tom Kyzer hostage and demanded a helicopter for your escape?"

My brain didn't seem to be functioning, but luckily everyone else's was. James and Danny closed in protectively on either side of me, each taking an arm, and they seemed to communicate with each other through nods as they led me through the crowd, batting away microphones and imposing camera lenses.

"What about the others?" I squeaked.

"They are right behind us," James growled, using his elbow to battle through the journalists. "Don't worry, it will be all right."

Despite his words, my heart sank when I realized how much trouble I was in. When Dad found out about all this, he was going to go crazy. I was meant to be keeping a low profile and now I had damaged our family's reputation even more and caused trouble for everyone. Connor had been right.

Everything was such a mess.

Danny let go of me to run forward and hail a taxi as we approached a main road. James gripped my arm even tighter, left alone to fend off the press on his own, while I hardly helped matters, tripping over the cobbles as we were moving so fast.

"Hey!" James said, as a tear rolled down my cheek. "You did really well, It Girl. Just concentrate on your balance, yeah? There are no duck ponds around here, but there are quite a few fountains."

James helped me into the car before slamming the door

behind me. The car waited as the boys ushered Jess and Stephanie into the back seats, and James instructed Jess over the noise to return to the hotel; the boys would follow in another taxi when one arrived.

The driver put his foot down and we sped away from the chaos.

"Well, I think it's safe to say that none of us expected you to do that." Jess breathed, a smile creeping across her face as she reached out and took my hand in hers. "Anna Huntley, you rock."

I had a sense that not everyone would feel that way.

18.

From: nicholas.huntley@bounce-mail.co.uk
To: anna_huntley@zingmail.co.uk
Subject: YOU ARE IN BIG TROUBLE

Anastasia Huntley, I am very disappointed in you.
What were you thinking? Not only did you
get yourself in trouble, but I can see from the
photos littered across every newspaper and
website on the planet that you led all your
friends into this mess too!

I don't know what you were doing away
from the hotel; your teacher has spoken to
me—yes, I've spoken to Mrs. Ginnwell, who of
course feels responsible for the whole thing,
even though I have assured her that I do not
blame her in the slightest because no doubt
you concocted some plan to mislead them—

and she has informed me that you will all be punished.

I told her that I was happy if she wanted to cut your stay short and put you on a plane back to England but she told me that wouldn't be necessary.

Thrown out of a stadium by security? Are you aware of the scrutinizing press attention we have got from this? Honestly, Anna, you're usually so sensible!

Well, some of the time.

Look, the main reason I am so angry with you is that something might have happened to you without an adult around to look after you in a strange city.

You have very much broken my trust, Anna.

That is why I am so angry.

We can talk about this properly when you get home, but for now STAY OUT OF TROUBLE.

That's a direct order.

Dad xx

From: helena@montaines.co.uk
To: anna_huntley@zingmail.co.uk
Subject: WELL DONE!

Darling Anna,

We are SO PROUD of you! I have just been in stitches laughing about all your scuffles with those large (and quite handsome) Italian security men!

If only I had spoken to you before the event: We discovered Marianne has been staying with some friends who live in the middle of nowhere and she's had no phone signal. Apparently she left a note on the fridge, but I can't think WHY she would think I would look there.

She knows I usually eat out.

Anyway, my heart simply swelled when I heard the news that you had snuck away and broken into the arena where Tom was playing! I knew straightaway you had gone there to tell Tom off and I think it's simply marvelous! And then you got thrown out! It's just like one of my old movies!

Ignore your father being grumpy—he has had a sense-of-humor failure. By the time you come home he'll be laughing along with the rest of us. And, you know, secretly he is impressed that his feisty little daughter went to all that trouble on Marianne's behalf.

Proud to officially call you my daughter in a few weeks.

All my love,

Helena xxx

From: rebecca.blythe@bounce-mail.co.uk
To: anna_huntley@zingmail.co.uk
Subject: Are you okay?

Darling Anna,

I've read all about it and I've spoken to your father and I just wanted to check in and make sure you're okay?

I don't condone you sneaking off like that, Anna, but I have to say I did chuckle when I saw those pictures of you being thrown out of the stadium. Nick's eyebrows really flew off his head! Just like that time he found out I had used his credit card to save a darling little donkey I saw starving away on one of those TV commercials.

Anyway, after all this malarkey in Rome, I'm looking forward to having you home. Dog is very much missing you, and your father tells me he's been acting in the most peculiar manner. He keeps howling at the moon, which is annoying the neighbors. (Dog, not your father.) You know Mrs. Trott who lives next door to you? The one with the very mean face who got in your dad's trash can? She's been terrifying your father because of it. He keeps hiding behind curtains when she walks past the house. She must have given him quite the lecture.

And, perhaps more strangely, Dog is currently insisting on sliding down the stairs on his back. He hasn't walked down them once the past few days, just lies down, rolls over, and propels himself down using his back legs to push off. I don't know if dogs can get carpet burn but Dog must have very thick hair on his back.

Anyway, darling, you were very naughty to
get into so much trouble and you mustn't
do anything like that ever again. But I'm also
proud of you for being so determined.
You get that from me, you know.
Love, Mom xxx

"Mrs. Ginnwell, please," I begged, "it really wasn't their fault. It was mine."

"That's not true—we volunteered," James jumped in. "We are as much to blame as Anna is. In fact, it was my idea in the first place."

"*James!*" I protested through gritted teeth, but he stood firm, looking straight at Mrs. Ginnwell and being as stubborn as she was.

Mrs. Ginnwell glanced at Mr. Kenton. We had been summoned to the lounge area where the four teachers were sitting waiting as the five of us were marched in. I had been adamant that I was going to take the fall for this one.

"James is right," Jess piped up, ignoring my glares. "We all played our part. If anything, Anna was trying to persuade us not to join in."

Mrs. Ginnwell nodded. "I have to say," she began, "I appreciate your honesty. What you did could have been extremely dangerous. You're in a strange city and none of us knew where you were. What if something had happened to you all? Did you think about that?"

"Of course," James replied firmly while I was still processing the question. "That's why we went as a team. We weren't going to let one go on their own. Safety in numbers."

"And it was just the five of you?" Mr. Crowne asked, looking more tired than concerned.

"Yes," I replied.

"We ask because I believe around the time that you snuck out of the hotel an incident occurred involving Miss Parker, Mr. Dakers, and a no-longer-in-one-piece vase." Mr. Kenton ran his eyes slowly along the row. "You wouldn't happen to know anything about that?"

"No, why? What happened?" Stephanie asked innocently.

"Just a coincidence, then?" Mr. Kenton said.

"Must have been." Danny shrugged.

Mr. Kenton looked suspicious, but then his shoulders relaxed. "Well, anyway, just the five of you, then."

He looked at Mrs. Ginnwell, who inhaled slowly, deciding our fate. She let out a long, heavy sigh. "I'm afraid as punishment I can't allow any of you to attend the end-of-trip party—"

"Mrs. Ginnwell," I interrupted, "if anyone has to be punished, it really should just be—"

"Anna," Stephanie said softly, shaking her head.

I pursed my lips.

"As I was saying," continued Mrs. Ginnwell, "you will not be able to attend the end-of-trip party, and instead you will spend tomorrow night writing an essay about Rome's beautiful landmarks, their background, architectural highlights, and what you have learned from them."

Jess groaned. Danny raised his hand.

"Yes, Danny?"

"Do we just discuss the ones we've seen, or should we add in other landmarks that are culturally significant, but which we haven't been able to fit into our itinerary?"

Jess hit him over the head while Miss Lawler gave a sigh of admiration.

"Whatever you wish, Daniel." Mrs. Ginnwell nodded. "Unless anyone has anything to add, you may all go to your rooms. Except you, Miss Huntley. Stay a moment."

The others filed out slowly, Jess mouthing, "We'll see you in a minute."

"I just wanted to check you were all right, Anna," Mrs. Ginnwell explained when the others had left. Having been concentrating on the patterns on the floor, too terrified to look at her, I raised my eyes.

"You wanted to check I was all right?"

"Yes." She gestured for me to sit down. "We were all worried."

I looked from her to Mr. Kenton, Miss Lawler, and across to Mr. Crowne, all of them watching me intently. "Uh. I'm fine."

"It can't be easy," Mr. Kenton began, "to be in such a position at your age. What you did was wrong, Anna—you should never sneak away again. But having to face that amount of paparazzi without an adult or anyone to guide you through it? It must have been terrifying on your own."

"I did have someone to guide me through it," I replied. "Four someones, in fact. I wasn't on my own."

"Right." Miss Lawler nodded. "You should know that we've spoken to the hotel and they are fully aware of the situation. They won't be letting any journalists on the premises."

"Thank you."

I waited in silence until Mrs. Ginnwell gestured that I could leave, and then, mumbling apologies again for everything, I scuffled out and hurried up to my room where Sophie was lounging on her bed wearing a bright green face mask.

"I take it, it didn't go well," she drawled, not even bothering to look up and flicking a page of a magazine as I collapsed onto my bed, suddenly exhausted.

I closed my eyes, burying my head further into the pillow.

"Connor called earlier by the way," she announced when I didn't say anything.

"Really?" I lifted my head and a wave of nauseating guilt washed over me. Connor had strictly told me not to do anything rash or get into trouble and I had managed to accomplish both. He must be so worried.

"He left a message." She licked her finger and turned another page of the magazine. "He said to tell you that the comic-book agent he's hoping to sign with wants a meeting and so he doesn't think he'll be able to make it to the airport when we land."

"Oh." I paused, my heart sinking. "Did he say anything else?"

"No, although I can't say I appreciated his tone when I gave him my opinion on comic books."

"Did he want me to call him back?"

"He didn't say."

I nodded. "Right. Thanks for passing on the message."

"Don't expect it to happen again—I'm not some kind of secretary," she huffed, putting down the magazine and sauntering into the bathroom to fill the tub with water.

"By the way, Sophie," I said, watching her dab at her face with a washcloth. "Thanks for helping out tonight."

"Whatever, it's not a big deal." She shrugged, continuing to wipe away the green mush. "I didn't do it to help you out—I just want an invite to the wedding reception."

"Either way, thanks."

She didn't respond. I pulled on my pajamas and slipped under the duvet, put it over my head, and wished it would just swallow me up.

19.

"ARE YOU JUST GOING TO SIT THERE?"

Sophie straightened up after digging around in her makeup bag, flicked her hair back, and then twisted it into a messy bun on the top of her head. Miraculously, even though it looked like she was receiving style tips from a pineapple, she also still managed to look like she'd just walked off a catwalk.

"Uh . . ." I turned the page of my book. "Yes?"

She opened the wardrobe and inhaled loudly through her nose as an artist might do before creating a masterpiece, staring at their canvas.

"Josie is going to come in here to get ready for the party," she informed me. "You might want to go read in Jess's room."

"We're not allowed. We have to stay in our rooms and write the essays on our own in silence." I looked back down at my book.

"All right, then, you can stay."

I was tempted to remind her that it was MY ROOM, but I still felt slightly indebted after she helped us escape from the hotel so I kept my mouth shut.

"Do you have your makeup and hair done professionally before all those events you go to?" Sophie inquired, separating hangers and inspecting the garments hanging from them. "I mean, you look way better at those sort of things than when you're, you know . . . just normal you."

"Thanks? Yeah, Marianne has a stylist who picks out what I'm going to wear and then someone sorts out my face and everything."

"That's really cool," she said with a smile. I smiled back and we held eye contact.

Oh my goodness. That was a moment.

SOPHIE PARKER AND I TOTALLY HAD A MOMENT. WE WERE BONDING.

I put my book down in case she wanted to give me a hug or something now that we were bonding.

"I mean, no offense, but you really need the help in the wardrobe department, you know," she said, holding up a dress and then throwing it on her bed. "You can tell when you've picked an outfit yourself. It's like a hobo vibe."

Maybe not.

There was a knock on the door and Sophie, without even looking at me, went, "Can you get that? It's not like you've got anything better to do," as she continued to hurl items onto her bed.

I dragged myself off the bed and opened the door to be greeted by Josie holding a pile of clothes and looking repulsed by my appearance. "What are you *wearing*?"

"A onesie."

"You look like a blueberry."

"It's an Eeyore onesie. You know, from *Winnie-the-Pooh*?" I turned and stuck out my bottom, giving it a wiggle. "See? It's got the tail. I have matching slippers too."

Seriously, why do I do things like wiggle my bottom at the most popular girls in school? WHY?

One day I am DETERMINED to act like a Normal Person.

Josie raised an eyebrow and Sophie looked at me in exasperation from where she was sitting. "I really didn't think you could get any weirder after the beetle comment at the beginning of the trip, but the butt wiggle just then?" She shook her head at me. "That was a low point for you."

"So, you were wrong about Marianne and Tom, then," Josie said smugly. "I thought you said they were moving in together."

"I was wrong," I told her curtly.

"Well, that's what happens when you date a rock star," she sighed, as though she were well versed in these matters. "It never ends well."

"Anyway, come on in, Josie," I said through gritted teeth, standing back to let her pass. "Make yourself at home."

"Whatever." She sauntered through and chucked the bag and all the clothes she was carrying across my bed.

"I'm actually sitting there," I said quietly, but was ignored as Josie launched into a speech about how she didn't have *anything* to wear and she hated *everything* she brought and thank *goodness* she had a friend like Sophie who could instruct her on what to do.

Wondering how on earth I had spent almost an entire semester putting up with Josie's whining—back when they thought being an It Girl meant I would immediately change personality and be their best friend—I carefully shuffled some of Josie's clothes down to the bottom end of the bed, slid under my duvet and picked up my book.

"Shall we do our makeup first?" Josie asked, getting out all her cosmetics and lining them up proudly along the dressing table.

Sophie nodded her approval of the plan and then the two of them began the process, perching neatly on stools and applying foundation to their already perfect skin.

"Tonight is going to be fun, right, Soph?" Josie began, filling the silence.

"Probably," Sophie replied indifferently, sifting through her pencils and picking up an eyeliner.

"Is Brendan coming here first so you can go to the party together?"

"No, I don't think so."

It wasn't the answer Josie was expecting, but she tried to play down her surprise. "Really? Why is that?"

"I don't know. We haven't talked about it."

"Is this about the fight you had last night?" Josie asked, lowering her voice to a whisper.

"What fight?"

"I heard you two had a big fight in the reception area . . . ," Josie said timidly. "You can tell me."

"Oh, that." Sophie's eyes met mine for the briefest moment in the reflection of the mirror. "Brendan was being totally immature and a massive drama queen and you know I don't have time for that. This trip has really opened my eyes. I decided it's time to break up. I want to date an older man."

"Urgh, yeah," Josie said, wrinkling her nose. "Boys our age are the worst. We need mature men."

I gaped at Sophie. She hadn't mentioned that she and Brendan had actually *broken up* last night. Does that mean that their fight was real? And the reason Sophie sounded so convincing during the whole thing was because she was actually being *honest*?

"Anna, why are you staring at us like that?" Josie sneered.

"I wasn't staring." I quickly looked down at my book. "I was just thinking."

Their next stage of preparation was wardrobe, and after what seemed like a hundred outfit changes, Josie settled on a very pretty short blue dress that Sophie picked out for her, and Sophie went with skinny black jeans and a cream embellished top with thin straps.

"Okay," Sophie sighed, picking up two pairs of shoes. "The main decision. Which pair? I like the black."

Josie nodded vigorously. "I love the black."

"But then I do like the green," Sophie mused.

"I LOVE the green," Josie agreed.

"So which pair?"

Josie blinked at her. "Er . . . which pair do *you* like?"

Sophie pursed her lips and then something strange happened.

"Anna," she commanded, "which do you like?"

I slowly raised my eyes from my book to see them both watching me, Sophie holding up the shoes, waiting for an answer, and Josie, whose expression had rapidly transitioned from stunned to furious.

"Sorry, are you talking to me?" I squeaked.

"Yes, stupid, I am talking to you. There are no other Annas in the room, thank God." Sophie rolled her eyes. "Which pair would you pick?"

I considered both pairs, looked her up and down and then said, "I'm not very good at this sort of thing, but I think the black ones." I paused. "If Marianne were here, she would go for the black ones with that sort of outfit. It's more sophisticated. I may be wrong. Like I said, I don't really know. I'll stop talking now."

Josie and I watched Sophie move over to her bed and sit down before sliding her feet into the black pair. She stood up and posed in front of the long mirror. "You're right, the black ones look good," she said simply.

Josie looked as though she had been slapped in the face.

"Are you ready, Josie?" Sophie asked, grabbing her clutch bag and throwing her phone and lip gloss in.

"I'll go get my bag," Josie mumbled. She eyed me suspiciously and then scampered out of the room.

I shook my head and went to put my book down on the bedside table when I saw the magazines about Helena and Dad, still stacked up there.

"Urgh," I groaned, tipping them onto the floor. "Why can't they just leave us alone?"

"A little bit of extra publicity never hurt anyone," Sophie declared, spritzing perfume onto her wrists.

"It does in this case," I replied. "I better phone my dad tonight. The whole Missing Marianne saga distracted me."

"Kind of proved my point, though, didn't it?"

"What did?"

"Tom and Marianne," she explained, spraying a loose tendril of her hair back into place. "Look, I'm not rubbing it in or anything. Just pointing out the facts."

"That was different," I said defensively.

"How?"

"Because . . . Tom is just a horrible person."

"Or maybe he's just a famous one." Sophie shrugged. "Like

you. And like your dad. It's just that he knows the score. Fame and love don't mesh well. That's just how it is."

"So, what are you saying? My dad's marriage is going to be a disaster?" I cried, exasperated. "That, because *I'm* famous now, I'll never get a happy ending either?"

"Hey," she said, holding up her hands so that all her bracelets tinkled down her delicate wrists, "don't shoot the messenger."

There was a knock on the door. "Sophie, are you ready?"

"Coming." She tucked her clutch bag under her arm, had one last mirror check, and tottered past my bed. "Good luck with the essay," she said breezily as she left, the door slamming behind her.

I picked up a magazine from the floor and looked glumly at the bold zigzags and heartbreak illustrations surrounding all the miserable-looking celebrities, Helena and Dad slap bang in the middle.

I was staring at it so hard for so long that when there was a gentle rap on my door I jumped out of my skin. Guessing that Sophie had forgotten something, I reluctantly opened the door, ready for the wave of perfume and hairspray to hit me in the face.

Instead, James slid into the room.

"Hey! What are you doing? They'll be around any minute to check on us."

"They're getting everything sorted for the party first. We've got a few minutes." He hesitated and ran his eyes from my head down to my feet. "Are you wearing a *Babygro*?"

"No!" I cried, the heat rushing to my cheeks. "It's a onesie. An Eeyore onesie. The donkey from *Winnie-the-Pooh*." I pulled at it nervously. "I wasn't expecting to see anyone."

James laughed and moved to go and sit where Sophie and Josie had been doing their makeup. "I wanted to check you were okay after speaking to the teachers on your own. I hope they weren't too mad at you. And also, in case you're regretting it, I wanted to remind you again that what you did was really cool. Throwing water over that idiot. He deserved it."

I smiled at his earnest expression. "Thanks. That's . . . really nice. Not that it made any difference—I think I just made everything worse. It was pointless anyway."

"What?" He furrowed his brow. "What do you mean it was pointless?"

I waved the magazine at him. "It was never going to work

between Tom and Marianne. Everyone else seems to know that. I should have just been realistic. Of course they broke up. After all, he is a rock star and she's . . ." I paused, my heart sinking. "She's an It Girl."

"So? What has that got to do with anything?" He gestured at the magazine in my hand. "You know better than anyone that those things are full of lies and rumors."

"Yeah, but they've got the gist of it, haven't they?" I felt the tears pricking at my eyes. "Relationships and all that stuff. It isn't real when you're famous."

"If that's your theory, you've proven yourself wrong." James stood up, walked over, and moved my feet so he could sit next to me on the bed.

"Tom has proven me right, you mean. Or proven Sophie right, anyway."

"Anna," he chuckled, "you sneaked out of a hotel; you risked getting in trouble to try and find your future stepsister; you bluffed your way into a rock star's concert to make sure that, *wherever* she was, she was okay; and you threw a jug of water over a jerk who was horrible about her when she didn't deserve it." He shook his head, bemused at my puzzled expression. "I think we can safely say that, famous or not, the way you feel about your family and friends is very real."

He picked up the magazine from my lap, rolled it tightly, and then lobbed it across the room and straight into the trash can before turning to look me in the eye.

"And same goes for the way we feel about you."

20.

JUST BEFORE WE WENT THROUGH ARRIVALS, MRS.
Ginnwell called us all into a group next to baggage claim and
made a long speech about how she hoped we'd had a truly
cultural experience that would stay with us for the rest of our
lives. It was really quite moving and I felt sad that our vacation
was over, despite all the crazy things that had happened—and
the fact that Connor hadn't been able to be there.

Then Sophie went and ruined the entire moment by asking if we could hurry things along as her dad was picking her
up and they had a dinner reservation to get to.

Letting Mr. Kenton lead the way through the arrival doors
where all our parents would be waiting, Mrs. Ginnwell asked
me to wait a moment. Jess, Danny, and Stephanie stopped
with me, and even James brought his trolley to a halt, knocking Brendan's arm and making him turn around too.

"Anna, I feel I should warn you—there is a horde of

paparazzi waiting for you through the arrivals doors."

"I should have guessed they'd know," I sighed.

"Miss Duke is there and I've just spoken to her on the phone. I believe your father has arranged for some airport security to help guide you to your car."

I nodded. Mrs. Ginnwell straightened up as two men and a woman in uniform came over to us. "Ah, here is the security. You might want to say good-bye to your friends so they can go through first."

"Thanks."

She smiled gently at me and then went to introduce herself to the security officers, who began to fill her in on the procedure of getting me safely to Dad's car.

Stephanie spoke first, walking around the trolley that had her and Danny's bags piled on it. "See you soon, Anna," she said with a smile, giving me a hug. "Thanks for the adventure."

"I'm so sorry I got you in trouble! And, because of me, you missed out on the party."

"Anna, we got kicked out of a show because you assaulted a rock star!" She grinned. "I've never had more fun in my life!"

I laughed and then held my arms out to say good-bye to Danny, attempting a ruffle at his blond curls, but he slapped away my hand just in time. "If you need a break from the wedding madness, let us know," he smiled, looking back at Stephanie and Jess, who were both nodding in agreement.

Jess moved forward and threw her arms around my neck. "See you, loser!"

She stepped back and pulled the sunglasses off the top of her head, gave the lenses a wipe with her T-shirt, and then put them on, turning to Stephanie and Danny. "I'm ready for the paps."

The three of them waved cheerily at me and then made their way toward the exit.

Brendan stepped forward and held up his hand for a high five.

"Nice work with my Genius Plan. I enjoyed plotting together," he said, then added, "I didn't think you had it in you, but I'll admit I was wrong. You've changed, Huntley. It's not every day that you take down a rock star."

"Thanks, Brendan." I laughed. "You're actually not the first person to say that about this trip. And you're not bad at acting. If ever you want to give it a stab, I could introduce you to Helena."

"It could be a good fallback if my football career doesn't work out," he considered. He looked at James, who was staring at his feet. "Well." Brendan rubbed his hands together. "I'm going to get out of here and leave you guys to it. Bye, Tyndale."

He clapped James on the back and then sauntered out, wheeling his suitcase behind him.

"So, guess I'll be seeing you back at school," James said.

"Guess so. Thanks for everything."

"I didn't do anything, Anna. Everything that happened, that was all you—I can't think of anyone else who would throw a jug of water in a jerk rock star's face."

I laughed and buried my face in my hands at the memory.

He pulled my hands away gently, standing so close that I went slightly cross-eyed, which probably wasn't my best look.

"I meant what I said about the fame thing, Anna. Don't worry about your dad or Marianne. It's not about them being famous—it's about knowing the right person at the right time. Your dad and Helena have that. Marianne will soon one day. And you . . ." Suddenly he let go of my hands and stepped back. "You have Connor."

"Thank you," I murmured.

"I better go," he mumbled. He grabbed the handle of his suitcase. "You don't need to thank me, Anna. You made my trip."

And with a weak smile, he waved good-bye and walked

toward the exit. I stood in a daze, trying to work out what on EARTH had just occurred. And trying very hard not to think about everyone I still needed to see at home.

"Right then," the security woman said chirpily behind me, making me jump about three meters in the air. "Are you ready to go?"

I gulped and nodded, searching frantically in my bag for my sunglasses and then putting them on. "I'm not being pretentious," I explained as one of the men took charge of my bag, coming to walk in front with Mrs. Ginnwell. The other two moved on either side of me. "I wear these so I don't get blinded by the camera flashes."

"No need to explain, Miss Huntley." The man next to me chuckled. "You just do your thing and let us do ours." He nodded at the woman and she placed an arm around my waist as he placed one around my shoulders.

The doors slid open, and the noise made my ears ring. Hundreds of flashbulbs went off and I just kept walking, putting my trust in the security officers. Eventually my head was ducked into a car and the door shut behind me.

My mom, waiting in the back seat, dragged me across into her arms, and Dad put his foot down hard on the accelerator, speeding away from the airport.

"We're so happy you're home!" Mom exclaimed, practically squeezing my face off my skull.

"Thanks, Mom," I wheezed, finally drawing breath when she released me. "Hey, Dad."

"Hello, Anna-pops. Glad you're home. By the way, you're grounded."

"What? *Why?* That is so unfair!"

"Hmm, let me think why you of all people might be grounded . . . ," he said, raising his eyebrows. "Perhaps it's because you disobeyed absolutely everyone, got thrown out of a music concert, and physically attacked a rock star. We're lucky he's not pressing charges."

"It was only water," I said huffily. "Helena said she was proud of me. Where is Helena anyway?"

"She's—" my mom began.

"She's busy," Dad said quickly.

I nodded. Dad changed the subject and I pretended I hadn't seen the warning look he gave my mom in the rearview mirror.

21.

DAD INFORMED ME THERE WAS A SURPRISE WAITING for me at the house.

I did all I could to get it out of him, questioning him the whole way home. "Is it a puppy? Is it? A little puppy? Did you get me a puppy?"

"No, Anna!" he cried as we turned into our road. "For the last time, it is NOT a puppy. Don't you think we have enough on our hands with your yellow Labrador? Last week Dog escaped, and then he came back carrying a cage with a parakeet inside it! It will be a long time before I even consider buying another dog."

My excitement vanished when I saw the swarm of paparazzi outside our house. Was this the surprise?

"Whoa." I gasped. "There are so many!"

"It's been like this all week," Dad seethed as they recognized the car and the camera flashes started popping. We crawled through them so Dad could park.

"Anna, look!" Mom laughed, pointing at the house.

Dog's head popped up at the window, and he started jumping up and down so excitedly when he saw the car that he actually headbutted the glass of the window as he sprang toward us and fell backward out of sight.

At first I thought he might have knocked himself unconscious, but then he sprang back into view, lunging at the glass again, headbutting it, and knocking himself backward for a second time.

"If he's not careful, he's going to kill himself," Dad said, parking and fumbling for the house keys. "Right, Rebecca, I'll come around and get the door on Anna's side and then we'll get her through them together."

"Yes, Captain," Mom said, saluting him.

He took a deep breath and then opened his car door and was hit with a barrage of noise. The door shut, muffling the sound again.

"Poor Dad. I feel terrible," I whispered, the guilt of my Italian adventure making my heart sink.

"This isn't your fault," Mom said gently. "It would have been like this no matter what happened. The wedding is a big story."

My door swung open. Dad helped me out and then tucked me under his arm, with Mom doing the same on the other side, and together we barreled through their microphones to the front door.

"Nick! Nick! Is it true the queen will be attending the wedding?"

"Nick! What do you have to say about claims the wedding may be canceled?"

"Anna, have you heard from Tom Kyzer after your heated row?"

As soon as we shut the door behind us, the three of us exhaled together and Dad shook his head, throwing the keys onto the telephone table.

"That was—"

But I didn't have time to finish my sentence. Dog zoomed out of the sitting room, skidded around the corner—taking down the telephone table, which crashed to the ground and sent the phone, books, and keys scattering—and ran full pelt straight at me, jumping up and crashing his head against mine.

I stumbled backward in a daze and then toppled over to

land on my back with Dog standing happily on top of me, slurping all over my face.

"Anna!" Mom cried. Dad grabbed Dog's collar and pulled him off me.

I instinctively rolled over onto my front.

"Anna, there is no need to get in the recovery position," Dad said in a strained voice, holding Dog's collar as he pulled with all his might to get to me.

"Are you all right?" Mom knelt down next to me and peered into my face.

"My face is broken," I groaned. "Tell me the damage! Will I ever be able to go out in public again?"

The corners of Mom's mouth twitched. "It looks like you're fine. Come on, up you get." She helped me to my feet and I cradled my face. "There you go," she said, guiding me forward. "Let's put you on the sofa with a nice cup of tea."

I hobbled into the sitting room and there, standing in the middle of it, waiting for me, was Connor.

"Surprise!" he said, stepping forward enthusiastically before stalling, clearly not sure what to do.

"Connor!" I cried, still holding my face. "You're here!"

We both stood awkwardly. "Shall I . . . uh . . . Are you okay? I heard a commotion."

"Oh, Dog tried to kill me. It's no big deal."

"I'll just go and help your father make the tea and leave you guys to get reacquainted," my mom said in this really embarrassing, smushy voice. "You must be so pleased to see each other! I remember the first time I saw Miguel after he left prison and—"

"OKAY, THANKS, MOM."

She nodded in understanding, backed out of the room, and then *winked* at me before shutting the door behind her.

Where can I get a new family?

"Sit down!" I said in an embarrassingly squeaky voice, breaking the silence and gesturing to the sofa. He sat down, pushing his gorgeously floppy bangs out of his eyes. I'd been looking forward to seeing him so much while I was in Italy and now here he was right in front of me on the sofa, and I was feeling . . . *nervous.*

That was a good thing, right? Looking at Connor, it seemed as if he might be feeling the same way.

"Sorry about my parents. Have you been waiting here long?" I said.

"I had Dog keeping me company," he said, the corners of

his mouth wrinkling into a shy smile. "He went bonkers when he saw you drive in."

"Yeah, I saw him at the window." I laughed.

We both went quiet again. "So, tell me about the comic book!"

"It's great! Really good. Thanks so much for your e-mails."

"That's okay. I'm sorry I wasn't here to cheer you on while it was all happening!"

"To be honest, I haven't really left my room," he explained. "I've had a lot on my plate."

"Sure," I agreed.

"So, Italy . . ."

"Oh, my goodness, Connor, it was just incredible. So hot over there and everyone is so fashionable and all the buildings are the most beautiful things. And the food—it's so good." I grinned at him. "I had a LOT of ice cream."

"And got into a *lot* of trouble." He raised his eyebrows. "I heard Tom Kyzer didn't enjoy his Italian experience as much as you did. I had a hard time believing what the press was saying had happened."

"Really?" I felt my cheeks flushing and wished we could talk about something else.

"It just didn't sound like you. I don't know." He hesitated

and then reached over and placed his hand over mine. "I'm just glad you're okay."

"I'm okay." I smiled. "Thanks."

"And I'm glad that you found the ice cream." Connor grinned.

I laughed. This felt a bit more like the "us" I was used to before I went to Italy. I figured we must both be feeling nervous after not having been able to talk much in Rome.

I felt a wave of guilt as I remembered what Sophie had said about Connor, who, despite his shy tendencies, put up with all the drama that came hand in hand with dating me, like having to battle through the paparazzi to get to my front door and face seeing pictures of himself plastered all over the Internet whenever we went on a date. And after the Tom Kyzer thing, all he cared about was that I was okay.

I realized I needed to make things okay again for good or I was going to lose not only someone who cared about me that much, but also potentially the ONLY person in the world who would put up with me doing stupid, embarrassing things like knocking over Iron Man and almost flattening everyone.

"Connor," I said, sitting up with a sudden brain wave, remembering something Helena had said before the vacation. "Will you come to the wedding with me?"

"The wedding? Your dad's wedding?"

"Yeah." I nodded firmly. "Will you come with me? Like as my, er, date. Obviously."

"Of course! That is, if you want me to."

"Yes. Yes I do want you to. Are you sure? Helena might make you walk me down the aisle and stuff—you know she's corny about that kind of thing." I laughed half-heartedly.

"No problem," he said, looking a bit taken aback but pleased nonetheless.

"Great!"

He nodded and it went back to silence again except for all the yelling outside from the reporters. They knew that we weren't going to come out again so I don't know why they had decided to raise their voices all of a sudden. Then the doorbell rang.

"Is that the press?" Connor looked flustered. "You don't ever get a break, huh?"

We heard Dad march down the hall and then, quick as a flash, open the door and shut it again. Dad greeted whoever it was and then I heard a familiar sound of clacking along our floor. I leaped to my feet as the sitting-room door opened.

"Marianne!" I cried, rushing over and throwing my arms around her.

"Hey there," she gasped as I pounced on her.

I took a step back and looked at her.

"How are you?" I asked.

"I've been better." She smiled weakly and I had to agree. Her eyes, usually defined with thick eyeliner, were red and squinty, with dark circles below them. I took in her tracksuit bottoms and loose-fitting sweater, her makeup-free face and jewelry-free wrists. She still looked more beautiful than anyone else I knew, though.

She waved her sunglasses in her hand. "Thank goodness for these. They cover my face so I won't look so horrific in the photos." Her eyes moved past me. "Hey, Connor, good to see you."

"You too."

He stood up and gestured for her to sit on the sofa while he went to sit in the armchair. I slumped down next to her and held her hand. "I'm so sorry about Tom, Marianne," I said gently.

"Me too," she replied, squeezing my hand.

Mom came in with biscuits and tea for everyone, and Dad followed her, bringing through Dog who ran over to give Marianne an enthusiastic welcome. She smiled and stroked his soft head as he put his paw up onto her lap.

Dog's sensitivity never fails to amaze me.

"I heard about what you did in Rome, Anna. Attacking Tom with a jug of water and being thrown out of the show," Marianne said, the corners of her mouth twitching.

"Ah, yes," I said, leaning back onto the cushions. "That old tale."

"I think the whole world knows," Connor commented.

"Marianne, I'm really sorry. I didn't mean—"

"That was the nicest thing anyone has ever done for me," she said, quietly interrupting me with a grateful smile. Her eyes filled with tears. "Thank you."

My mom gave out a little sob and Dad rolled his eyes.

"Um, I should probably be going," Connor said suddenly.

"Really?" I tried not to sound too surprised.

"I've had a long break from work and I've got a bit to do. Plus," he glanced at Marianne, "I should let you guys catch up."

"I'll drop you home, Connor," Dad said. "You don't want that lot outside pestering you."

"I'll do it, Nick," Mom insisted. "You relax for a bit."

Connor thanked them and then said good-bye to Marianne. We followed Mom into the hall. "We had better link arms, Connor, and face them together," she sighed.

He nodded and then turned to me.

"I'll call you tonight," he promised. "We'll do something over the next couple of days. I really do want to hear all about your trip. It'll be just like old times."

I smiled.

Conscious that we weren't alone, he leaned over, gave me a peck on the cheek, and then walked out with Mom into the chaos.

22.

EXACTLY ONE WEEK BEFORE THE WEDDING I ASKED
Dad when the rehearsal would be.

"What rehearsal?" he responded, not looking up from his computer as I peered around the door of his study.

"The wedding rehearsal. You know, where we run through everything. Practice walking down the aisle and that sort of thing."

"Oh, that. We won't be doing that." He continued to type furiously at his keyboard.

I folded my arms. "Why not?"

"It's not necessary."

"It is very much necessary!"

"Anna," he sighed, finally turning to pay attention to me. "What is wrong? Can't you see I'm in the middle of something?"

"I just think it's weird not to have a rehearsal. How will I know how to walk down the aisle?"

"You just walk normally. I know it's hard for you but give it a go."

I narrowed my eyes at him. He turned back to his computer, but I didn't budge, studying his disheveled state. He was hunched over his desk wearing his blue-striped nightgown, his hair sticking up at all sorts of angles—clearly the victim of frantic hands—and the dark circles under his eyes more prominent than they had been.

"Hey, Dad, maybe we should both take Dog for a walk today."

"I've already arranged for Sam down the road to do it," he answered, dismissing my suggestion with a wave of his hand. "It would be chaos if we tried."

"The photographers aren't *that* bad."

"HA!" He shook his head and then reached for the phone before dialing a number and then looking up at me. "Off you go now. I have lots to do."

I let out a long sigh so that he knew I was annoyed—not that he noticed—and then I shut the door to his study and went to the sitting room, where Marianne was crouched over the chessboard, Dog lying next to her on his back with his legs splayed and his tongue lolling out.

As she was still finding the breakup hard and couldn't face the public quite yet, she was spending a lot more time at our house, enjoying the peace and quiet of being cooped up, unlike me.

Her forehead was creased in concentration. "You know," she said thoughtfully, rubbing Dog's belly, "I'm pretty sure that you can't just move your pieces any old way. I think there are rules about that. Like only certain pieces can move in certain ways."

"Nah," I said innocently, coming to sit opposite her. "That is stupid. You're just saying that because I'm winning."

She lifted her eyes. "So, what did your dad say about the rehearsal? When is it?"

"He said there isn't one."

"Why is your face weird?"

"What do you mean?" I said defensively. "This is my face."

"I mean, your expression. You look concerned."

"It's just . . ." I bit my lip. "Dad's acting a bit strange. That's all."

"So is Mom," Marianne informed me. "She's been spending

a lot of time chatting quietly to Fenella and people on the phone. I told her to come here, but she said she didn't want to draw any more attention to this house. I guess she's really busy sorting last-minute plans."

"Dad hasn't left the house in days," I huffed. "He's scared of the paps."

"He's going to have to get used to it. I thought he would be by now."

"It is a lot more intense with the wedding," I said, moving to the window and peeking past the curtain at all the journalists standing around our pathway, chatting among one another, flicking cigarette stubs onto the pavement, and checking their phones every few seconds. "You'd think they'd get bored."

"A wedding this big? No way. They won't risk missing a minute."

"I'm worried about Dad. I want to help." I sat down again. "Do you think we should do something?"

She moved her queen and then gestured for me to take my turn. "What do you mean?"

"I don't know." I rested my head in my hands. "Something to get rid of that lot outside." I nodded toward the window.

"Like that's going to happen," Marianne snorted.

"I'm being serious!"

"So am I. It's just part of the deal, isn't it?" she said, picking dog hairs off her jeans.

"What deal? I don't remember there ever being a deal? Did I sign something?"

"Not like that, dummy." She chuckled, rolling her eyes. "As in, it comes hand in hand with what we do."

"I don't see why," I said huffily.

"Don't you? I do. Mom needs the press to be successful in the film industry. As annoying as they are," she said, jerking her head, "it's also thanks to them that she has had publicity for her work. And it's thanks to them that I have been able to promote certain brands and campaigns. We're in the public eye and, because of that, certain opportunities come our way. You *know* all this."

"I just never thought they would be so interested in my dad. It's not like he's a celebrity. I don't think he was prepared for all this attention."

"He should have been." She shrugged. "He's marrying my mom. He knew what he was getting himself into."

"It's quite intimidating."

"Well, yeah, I guess it's worse at the moment, but you've gotten used to it, haven't you? So has your dad, I'm sure."

"But, Marianne . . ." I paused, choosing my words carefully.

"With you and Tom"—I saw her wince—"do you think if you weren't famous it might have worked out?"

Her face contorted and I regretted asking it at once.

"Sorry," I said quickly. "Forget it. Let's just play chess." I stared at the board and then moved my castle.

"In answer to your question, I don't know," she said quietly. "Maybe it would have been easier if we weren't pestered all the time. Maybe if he hadn't been famous, he wouldn't have met Natalia. Maybe I was just wrong about who he was." She sighed heavily. "The thing is, Anna, it's easier not to ask that question. This is the world I'm in whether I like it or not. I'll never be able to have a relationship without the fame that comes with it. I'm an It Girl—it's who I am. And now so are you."

She reached over the board, lifted her bishop, and then placed him down in another square.

"Checkmate."

"Impossible," I protested. "Bishops can only move backward and they're only allowed on the black squares."

"You're just saying that because I won." Marianne held my king up victoriously in the air.

Not one to miss an opportunity, Dog suddenly scrambled to his feet and jumped at her, grabbing the king in his jaws, throwing back his head, and swallowing it all in one. He licked his chops and then hopped up onto the sofa, nestling happily into the cushions.

"Well," Marianne said, "I think we don't need to argue anymore over who the winner is in this situation."

We both burst into laughter and Dog let out a triumphant burp.

The next day, Connor wanted to go to the park together, but there was no way we could have gone somewhere so open, not at the moment. I felt awkward about it being so complicated, especially when he was so busy with his drawing, and I did wonder whether we should just cancel the date altogether and leave it until we saw each other on the day of the wedding.

But then he made the suggestion that I come over and check out his new comic book, which seemed like the perfect solution for both of us: It meant he wouldn't have to take too much time off from working, plus we'd be in private so he could see me without having to worry about being the top hit on a showbiz gossip website.

I also wanted to talk to him about my dad, who had been so quiet lately, hiding away in his study and brushing away any questions I had about the wedding. Even something as simple as asking whether Mom was going to drop me at Helena's on the day so I could get ready with Marianne. I had no idea what was going on or what he was feeling—although he was clearly feeling anger when Dog vomited the chess piece up in his study a few minutes after consuming it.

"Look at this, Anna," he said in a disgusted voice, showing me an opinion column in a newspaper. "All that space dedicated to *guessing* at how the Tilney Hotel is preparing for the wedding. It's not even fact! The writer admits he hasn't had any contact with them! He *believes*, however, that they will be doing all this. Oh, well, it must be right, then." He shook his head. "What a waste of a perfectly good column. I've met that journalist—he's an intelligent man. What a waste," he repeated, angrily buttering his toast and sending crumbs flying everywhere, much to Dog's delight who snapped ferociously at them like edible confetti.

"You don't care about this stuff, right?" I asked nervously, putting the paper to one side. "It doesn't affect the wedding or, you know . . . the marriage. It will be really great. The Tilney is perfect for you and Helena. The perfect wedding."

"Yeah," he said, shifting uncomfortably.

"One week away now, Dad," I began tentatively, watching

him closely. "One week until you become a married man."

He didn't say anything. He just took a bite of his toast, went, "I've got to get on with things," and then walked out of the room with Dog in hot pursuit of crumbs.

I bit my nails anxiously as I relayed all this to Connor.

"He's probably busy with wedding stuff. I wouldn't worry, Anna. Maybe you're overthinking?"

I chewed my lip. Connor was probably right. He knew how worried I was about Dad. But something still wasn't quite right with the whole situation. If only I could put my finger on it—

"So, what do you think of her hair color? Do you think it works?"

"Sorry? Whose?" I looked at what Connor was pointing at on the page. "Oh."

Ember, the heroine of *The Amazing It Girl*, was running through the streets of London in pursuit of someone who had stolen government secrets.

"She's . . . blond." I looked up at Connor, trying not to sound hurt. She had originally been a redhead, inspired by the hair color I chose to change to after Dad had announced his engagement and I was suddenly being photographed all the time.

"Yeah. The red worked for the first book, but you have to mix things up, I think," he said, shuffling some paper around on his desk and pulling out another one for me to see.

I nodded. "She looks great. Maybe I should go blond," I quipped. Connor smiled but didn't say anything.

"Do you think the storyline works? I'm not sure if it's too obvious, like it's been done before," he said anxiously. "Is it too bland?"

"It's a good storyline," I assured him. "It's fast-paced, action-packed, and has brilliant characters. I love that the main suspect is Ember's childhood friend, a good clash of emotions. Your agent will love it and it will become a huge hit."

He held the drawings tightly in his hands. "I hope so."

I couldn't help smiling at his creased forehead and dark furrowed eyebrows as he examined his work closely. I loved seeing him so passionate about the comic, even if it did mean it was all he ever talked about.

"Sorry," he said when I got my stuff ready to leave, "this can't have been the most fun date for you."

"Don't be silly—it's my fault. Once the wedding is out of

the way, it will go back to normal." I nodded cheerily.

"What do you mean?" He looked confused.

"Well, the press," I said, wondering what else it could be.

"But," he began, his brown eyes fixed on mine, "it was never . . . normal."

"No, I know, but I mean it won't be so bad," I explained. "We can just carry on like we were."

He hesitated. "You don't think it will get easier, do you?"

"Of course it will!" I exclaimed, baffled that he didn't get it. "After the fuss of the wedding, they'll lose interest and move on to the next thing."

"Anna," he said gently, "I don't think that's going to happen. If anything, it will get worse. Your dad will be married to Helena Montaine. You'll move and be the stepdaughter of the most famous actress in the world. And, yeah, your dad is of interest to them because he's Helena's husband, but the world will be way more fascinated by you and Marianne. They'll be watching you every step of the way. Two It Girls under one roof?" He shook his head and exhaled. "It's a reporter's dream."

But before I could say anything Connor's mom interrupted to tell us that the car had arrived to pick me up.

* * *

That night it took me a long time to fall asleep. I was starting to think Sophie could have been right about everything, but I buried my head in my pillows and told myself that I would feel different in the morning. I would talk to Dad first thing and all would be well.

But it turned out he had other plans.

23.

SOMEONE WAS SHAKING ME. I BATTED THEM AWAY
and rolled over into my pillow.

"Anna! Anna!" The shaking began again.

Half asleep and trying to work out what was going on, I
opened my eyes to see my dad standing over me with a flashlight. "What the . . . Dad?"

"Come on, it's time to get up."

"What?" I squinted at my clock. "No, it's three a.m."

"Up you get. Put this on." He was holding out one of my
sweaters.

"Have we been called up to the secret service or something? That's the only reason I can think of as to why I'd be
up this early. Did the queen call?"

"Just put your sweater on and don't turn on any of the
lights."

"Look, Dad, clearly you're having some kind of mental

breakdown. And I wanted to talk to you about this whole thing and it's important to—"

"We can talk another time, Anna," he said, placing my sweater on my bed and leaving the room. "Just get dressed and come downstairs. Remember, no lights."

I pulled my sweater on, swung my legs out of bed, and stretched before plodding out in my slippers and treading very carefully down the stairs in the pitch black. Feeling the walls to guide me along, I followed them into the kitchen, where I could see the pool of light on the floor from a flashlight.

"Hey, Anna," I heard a voice say from one side of the room.

"Sam?"

The flashlight moved so that it lit up the face of our neighbor. "Howdy," he replied. In the light, I could see Sam was holding a plate of ham and throwing a bit at a time to Dog, who was sitting obediently next to him, a pool of drool at his paws.

"What is going on?"

"Sam is here to look after Dog. We're distracting him with ham so he doesn't bark when we go," Dad whispered, shining the light into my eyes and frazzling my retinas.

"Go where? What is going on? Why am I awake?"

"I'll explain in a bit," Dad said, before moving the light back to rest on Sam's face. "I've parked around the corner so we'll go out the back. I've written everything down."

"Don't worry, Mr. Huntley." He grinned. "I'll hold the fort. They won't suspect a thing." He happily tossed another bit of ham in the air for Dog.

"Thank you. Come on, Anna, we're going out the back. Take my hand, please."

Before I had time to ask once again what on earth was going on, Dad grabbed my hand and pulled me through the kitchen and out the back door, following the path around the side of the house. He raised a finger to his lips and pointed at all the cars parked nearby with sleeping journalists in the front seats. Then he switched off the flashlight and we hurriedly walked down the road without saying a word.

Since Dad was clearly in a VERY fragile state I decided not to say anything until we were in the car and Dad had jabbed the keys to the ignition and begun driving, his eyes wide and bright with adrenalin. He honestly looked like he'd just escaped from prison.

"Dad." I held up my hands, feeling very alert now after my early-morning wake-up call. "I appreciate that you are going through a lot of stuff right now and your stress levels are through the roof and, don't get me wrong, I am kind of enjoying the little Famous Five–type adventure with a bit of *Shawshank Redemption* thrown in that we're having right now, but I think that you need to pull over and we need to have a talk about everything. I want you to know that it's okay that you've completely lost your mind. We can talk it through and I will *probably* not tease you about what's just happened. I say probably because I can't make any promises. Especially with your hair looking like it is. You look like the creepy, mad professor on those cereal boxes. I'm just saying it how it is."

"It's okay, Anna," Dad said excitedly, speeding down the empty roads that would be rammed with traffic at a normal hour. "Everything will make sense in a moment. Here, let's listen to some radio."

He turned on some music and did the weirdest thing. He began to hum. *HUM.* And not in an absentminded kind of way either, but in a really cheery way.

He really had lost his mind.

Speechless, I just watched the blurred street lamps out the window, baffled by my father's behavior. I didn't even notice where we were going until he slowed down and pulled into the car park of a very swanky hotel.

"Dad—"

"Come on," he interrupted, getting out of the car, slamming the door, and passing the keys to the valet, who greeted him as though he'd met him before.

I got out, suspiciously eyeing up the valet—who pretended not to be weirded out by the way I was staring at him—and followed my dad through the large doors of the hotel, opened for us by a man wearing a top hat and tails.

"Good morning, Miss Huntley," he said cheerily, touching the brim of his hat. "Welcome to the Dashwell Hotel."

"Er. Yeah. Hey," I mumbled back, instinctively mirroring him, but I forgot I wasn't wearing a hat so I just touched the top of my head for no reason.

I stepped into the lobby of the hotel and immediately regretted the fact that I was still in my pajamas and Eeyore slippers. I obviously knew the Dashwell. Everyone knows the Dashwell. It is one of London's oldest, most beautiful hotels and it was grander than any place I've ever been to—and, considering I hang out with Helena Montaine, that's really saying something.

I hurried to catch up with my dad who was talking to the smiling receptionist and, in my haste, skidded across the marble floor, slamming right into his back. "Dad—"

"I'll be with you in a second, Anna," he dismissed, continuing his conversation.

Eventually he turned around and passed me a heavy, gold room key. "Here you go—that's yours."

A young man wearing a smart blue gold-buttoned uniform with his hair tucked under a matching blue hat came out of nowhere and was suddenly by my side, telling me that he was going to show me to my room.

"I'm at the other side of the hotel." Dad grinned, wiggling his key in his hand. He bent down and gave me a kiss on the head. "See you later, Anna-pops."

He spun me around and gave my back a firm poke with his finger so I tripped over my feet following the guy, who had launched into a monologue about the history and heritage of the hotel, pointing out famous artworks as we passed them.

I blame the fact that I was so compliant with all this on tiredness. Had I been a little more alert I would have certainly thrown something at my dad's head before this stage and forced him to tell me what was going on.

"And here is your room," the man gestured. "Would you like help with your key?"

I didn't need to answer, though, because the door we had stopped at swung open and a pair of arms reached out and pulled me in, enveloping me in a warm embrace while the hotel attendant stood by.

"Thank you, sir!" I heard Marianne say as she held on to me and the door creaked shut. She pulled back to hold me at arm's length. "Well, hello there, droopyface."

"CAN SOMEONE PLEASE TELL ME WHAT IS GOING ON?" I yelled.

"You haven't worked it out already?" She squished my cheeks and then walked through our suite—which, by the way, was the size of the whole bottom floor of our house and was adorned with huge bouquets of flowers and large wicker baskets of exotic fruit. I felt like I was in a twisted modern-day version of *Alice in Wonderland*.

I padded after Marianne, who suddenly stopped and pointed at something in the corner. Hanging up in the walk-in wardrobe, taking up the majority of the space in it, was a large ball of purple frilled silk and netting.

"What is my bridesmaid dress doing here?"

"Well," Marianne checked her watch, "in a few hours, once you've had your beauty sleep, you'll need to get into it."

I gaped at her, the truth finally dawning on me.

She grinned. "It's wedding time."

24.

THE CRAZIEST THING HAS HAPPENED.

Okay, so you know how the wedding is next week at the Tilney Hotel? IT IS SO NOT NEXT WEEK AND IT IS NOT AT THE TILNEY.

I am freaking out. Dad kidnapped me this morning and took me to where the wedding is really happening. And it's TODAY.

This is not a drill. I repeat. Not a drill.

Can you believe he organized this without telling me anything? Marianne says she had no idea either and she was also kidnapped this morning. Dad and Helena kept it

between themselves. And the hotel. And
the wedding team. And all the guests.
Including Connor. Who, by the way, didn't
say a word.

Hang on. Come to think of it, I'm pretty sure
I'm the last to know.

HOW COME I'M THE LAST TO KNOW?

As if Dad told people like Kanye West so
he could change his flights, yet he thought
I, his beloved daughter, was better off not
knowing. I am excellent at keeping secrets,
like that time he told me about the mishap
with my birth certificate. I haven't told a
SOUL.

Anyway, the point is that they've gone to all
this effort to trick the press!

It's incredible! They figured out the whole
thing while we were in Rome—they helped
all the guests to change their plans and even
got the Tilney Hotel to play along. Helena has
promised to have her next birthday party there,
so they were happy.

I would have called you to tell you both about this but there's a hundred people in my room setting up to do our hair and stuff.

I've escaped downstairs while Marianne is being shimmied into the makeup chair. But I'm up next so make your replies snappy.

Love, me xxx

From: jess.delby@zingmail.co.uk
To: anna_huntley@zingmail.co.uk
Cc: dantheman@zingmail.co.uk
Subject: Re: !!!

Wow! That's so cool!

By the way, what do you mean mishap with your birth certificate?

J x

From: anna_huntley@zingmail.co.uk
To: jess.delby@zingmail.co.uk
Cc: dantheman@zingmail.co.uk
Subject: Re: !!!

I just told you all that and you're concerned

with my birth certificate? Really? That's your priority here?

DID YOU READ THE REST OF THE E-MAIL?

From: jess.delby@zingmail.co.uk
To: anna_huntley@zingmail.co.uk
Cc: dantheman@zingmail.co.uk
Subject: Re: !!!
Seriously, though, what mishap on your birth certificate?

J x

From: dantheman@zingmail.co.uk
To: jess.delby@zingmail.co.uk
Cc: anna_huntley@zingmail.co.uk
Subject: Re: !!!
Wow. There are so many capital letters in this e-mail chain.

Danny

From: anna_huntley@zingmail.co.uk
To: dantheman@zingmail.co.uk

Cc: jess.delby@zingmail.co.uk
Subject: Re: !!!
SERIOUSLY, DANNY? THE FONT STYLE IS
WHAT HAS CAPTURED YOUR ATTENTION?

From: jess.delby@zingmail.co.uk
To: anna_huntley@zingmail.co.uk
Cc: dantheman@zingmail.co.uk
Subject: Re: !!!
So I just tried thinking about what mishaps
might occur on a birth certificate and I have
come up with the following list:
1. Wrong date
2. Wrong name
3. Wrong sex
4. Wrong parents
Which is it?
J x

From: dantheman@zingmail.co.uk
To: jess.delby@zingmail.co.uk
Cc: anna_huntley@zingmail.co.uk

Subject: Re: !!!
Let us hope it is point 1 or point 2.
Otherwise, things could get complicated.
Danny

From: anna_huntley@zingmail.co.uk
To: jess.delby@zingmail.co.uk
Cc: dantheman@zingmail.co.uk
Subject: Re: !!!
This reminds me. I forgot to make new friends
in Rome.

"Do you know what I feel like?" Marianne sighed as three members of Fenella's wedding team carefully pulled the heavy dress over her curlers and then yanked it down before kneeling beside her and getting lost in the layers of netting trying to arrange it properly.

"A giant cupcake."

"No, you look more like an upside-down hot-air balloon," I said thoughtfully, looking down at my matching disaster of a dress. "Or some kind of pufferfish. Or perhaps a purple profiterole?"

I turned around and the swish of all that material spinning

at such force knocked one of the wedding team engrossed in my skirt right over. I apologized profusely as the hairdresser came over to take out my curlers, and then she was let loose with the hair spray, putting every stray hair carefully into place.

Fenella declared us to be fit for a royal ball, and now that we were ready and it was time to beautify the bride, she snapped her fingers at the army of makeup, hair, and dressing professionals, who gathered up their crates of products and filed out of the room to make their way to Helena. She ordered Marianne and me to stay in our bedroom and not move.

Marianne grinned. "I can't wait to see Mom." She picked up her phone and sat down on the bed, her dress ballooning up around her. She tried to push down the swathes of material. "It's like some sort of weird duvet. I feel very padded. If some rugby player tackled me, they would bounce right off."

"I still can't get over the fact that they changed the wedding to today." I shook my head. "It doesn't feel real."

"Yeah, it's really cool. All those reporters still camping outside our houses are going to be so angry." She nodded. "No wonder Mom and Nicholas have been so stressed. They've been reorganizing the biggest wedding of the year right under the paparazzi's nose."

"It suddenly explains a lot," I agreed. "Although . . ." I trailed off into thought.

"What?" Marianne prompted.

"It's just, well, like you say, they went to a lot of effort and through so much stress just to avoid the press. My dad hasn't been himself at all." I paused. "Is this how it's going to be for the rest of our lives?"

Marianne snorted. "Why, how many celebrity weddings are you planning?"

I smiled and she shook her head, bemused, turning back to her phone and resuming her texting. I tried to distract myself. But all the worries that had been building up all summer were crowding my brain, and I couldn't stop myself from wondering whether Dad had really thought it all through.

Did he really know what he was getting himself in for? He *hates* the paparazzi and has changed his whole wedding just to escape them. But by marrying Helena Montaine he's never going to escape them properly. Sure, for a day or two, but they'll always be there lingering, waiting to get a good photo.

I thought of everything Connor had said. This wedding was just the beginning.

With no time to explain, I bundled up my skirt, stood up, and ran from the hotel room, ignoring Marianne's confused cries after me.

I had to talk to Dad before it was too late.

25.

"ANNA, WHAT ON EARTH IS GOING ON?"

I could kind of understand why Dad was confused. I mean, in very quick succession I had:

1. Shouted his name as I came barging into the main reception.
2. Made the mass of guests all look up from their champagne.
3. Stopped the jazz band midway through one of their melodies.
4. Bulldozed through the crowd when I spotted my dad on the other side of the room.
5. Which, when I'm wearing a dress the size of Mount Kilimanjaro, would terrify anyone.
6. Dragged him away without any explanation.

7. Taken him up the stairs to the first floor in the hope of finding a space where we could be alone.

8. And, when I couldn't find one, pushed him through the fire escape and onto the steps.

"What is your thing with fire escapes recently?" he asked, baffled. "Anna, you're acting very weird. Whatever it is you have to say, spit it out."

"Dad . . ." I hesitated as I took in his slightly disturbing lilac waistcoat that had clearly been chosen by Helena. I shook my head and pulled back my focus.

"Dad," I repeated, "are you sure about this?"

"Anna, what are you talking about?"

"Are you sure about this—the wedding?"

Dad looked at me as though I had lost my mind. "Of course I'm sure. What makes you think I'm not? Anna," he reached out to take my hand, "is everything all right? Maybe this is from lack of sleep."

I nodded. "Yes, I'm all right." Then I shook my head. "No. Wait. I'm not."

I couldn't stop myself and just like that the words spilled

out. Everything I had been worrying about the ENTIRE summer just exploded from me in one big long rambling speech where I barely paused for breath:

"If you marry Helena, you're going to spend the rest of your life dealing with reporters and photographers. Not just for big events like a wedding but for every tiny thing you do; every decision you make is going to be watched and commented on by the whole world. Some people just can't handle that, and it's okay if you can't. Recently, you've been acting strange and I think it's because of the pressure of the paparazzi and of being . . . well . . . famous. And also rearranging the wedding in a matter of weeks. But the fuss and the pressure aren't going to stop when this day is over. It will carry on for the rest of your life. And I'm worried."

Dad raised his eyebrows. "Let me get this straight. You're worried that I might not be aware of all that?"

"No. Yes. I don't know. I just wanted you to be absolutely sure. Because it's easy to get caught up in something, like falling in love with a glamorous movie star. But that doesn't mean it's *real*."

"Anna." Dad held up his hands. He sat down on the top step of the fire escape and motioned for me to join him. I tried my best to sit next to him but the width of my dress rendered this impossible, and in the end he had to sit a few steps down to make way for all the material. "Why don't you tell me what this is all about?"

I sighed and looked out at the view. It was kind of beautiful actually. From the fire escape you could see quite far across London which, from up there, seemed incredibly tranquil and still. There were no sandwich-stealing pigeons in sight.

"In Rome, someone was talking about how you can't really fall in love when you're famous. How celebrity relationships never work out. It's always in magazines, you know. Who is dating who, who is breaking up with who. It's like a game. They're not real. The pressure of fame always destroys anything good. Just like with Marianne and Tom."

Dad nodded slowly. "I see."

"I'm sorry, Dad," I continued. "I just want you to be ready for everyone to always want to stick their nose in your business and turn it into gossip. You hate that. That's why you've been distant recently, right? And now you're signing up for a lifetime of it."

"Yeah, I am." He shrugged. "Because I love Helena."

"But—"

"No 'buts'—that's all that matters. That's it." He smiled up at me, his eyes squinting as the sun shone down on the steps.

"The fame bit of things, yeah, it's annoying. And, yes, it is a huge pressure and some people can find that very hard. But the thing is, fame only gets in the way if you let it. If anything *isn't* real, it's the fame. How I feel about Helena—that's real."

"So, you're not worried at all?"

"About my private life being splashed around the papers? Of course. But that's what I signed up for when I started dating a film actress. That's what they see, the photographers and the reporters. They see a film actress and they want photos of her and what she's up to and who she's dating and who she's breaking up with." He put a hand on my foot that was poking out from the mound of netting. "I don't see a film actress—I just see Helena."

I nodded. "So, you don't think the fame thing will get in the way of, you know, your relationship?"

"No!" He laughed. "I've never doubted for one second what I was getting into. Even when I had to rearrange a wedding for hundreds of guests just a few weeks before the big day."

"You've been acting so strange that I thought the reality of being involved with someone famous was dawning on you," I admitted. "I was worried you had realized that it wasn't perfect and everything was going wrong."

"Things aren't perfect—they never are. Look, Anna-pops,

Helena might dress you up in quite frankly *ridiculous* fairy-tale dresses"—he ruffled my skirt—"but our relationship isn't a fairy-tale one. We have to work hard, but that's okay. We won't let anything get in the way, least of all the press."

"Really?"

"Really."

"So . . . this is the real deal. You're ready?"

"I'm ready."

I nodded. "Okay, then. You can go and get married now."

I smiled at him and then started preparing to hoist myself up from the step, which was going to be difficult with all the extra netting weight I was carrying, but Dad stopped me.

"Wait," he said sternly. "Are you sure everything's all right? There's nothing else you want to talk about?"

"Like what?"

"I don't know—any questions about the future or uh, well, your . . . um . . . love life?"

"GROSS, DAD, NO."

"What? Why is that gross?" Dad asked, feigning ignorance. "A dad is allowed to ask these kinds of questions."

"Uh, I think you'll find that a dad is NEVER allowed to ask those kinds of questions without clear, indisputable permission. I certainly have not granted such liberties."

"Okay." He held up his hands. "If you say so. But I'll leave you with this thought."

"Oh no," I groaned. "Are you going to quote a dead person? I really regret kidnapping you from your wedding. If I'd known I was going to get a lecture—"

"No," he said, all defensive, "I was actually going to try something original."

"Go on, then," I sighed, "and make it snappy. I've wasted enough of your time and I'm more worried about Fenella killing me than Helena if we muck up the schedule."

"Sometimes in life . . . let me finish, this is good advice," he argued, having caught my very deliberate eye roll. "Sometimes in life, things don't always go to plan. Things you thought you had all worked out, sometimes they're just not meant to be, it's not the right time or the right person and you have to let them go. But when something is worth fighting for, you fight for it. And you'll know when it is. Does that make sense?"

"I think so." I eyed him suspiciously.

"That's all, then." He got to his feet and then, using all the strength in his body, he hauled me up. "I'm guessing you didn't think to prop open the fire escape door with anything and now it's locked."

A sudden chill ran through me. "Oh," I whispered.

"Come on, then." He grinned, looking hardly concerned at all. "We'll have to go down the fire escape. I would offer to hold your hand as we go, but I have a feeling you've done this before."

"Very funny," I muttered, trying to make my way down the steps without tripping on the bottom of the dress and rolling the whole way down like a purple snowball.

"That dress, by the way, is completely absurd," Dad commented as we neared the bottom. "I've never seen anything like it. What was she thinking?"

"It's rather unusual," I agreed as he held out his hand to help me down the last few steps. "Suits our family, I guess."

"You can go around the back. There's an entrance through the courtyard. Might be easier to rejoin the ladies there. I'll go around the front and get into position."

He stood up straight and adjusted his tie. "How do I look?"

"Like John Wayne without the cowboy hat."

He beamed at me. "That will do!"

"Good luck, Dad. I'll see you in there."

"Anna," he said quietly, reaching for my hand. "Thank you."

"For saying you looked like John Wayne?"

"No. For checking."

I didn't know what to say so I just nodded.

He smiled and his eyes looked suspiciously shiny for a moment. "I'm proud of you, Anna."

"I'm proud of you, too, Dad." I patted his arm. "No need to get all mushy about it."

I watched him leave and then hurried toward the courtyard, hearing the chime of Big Ben in the distance. Helena would be coming down any moment, and Marianne was no doubt panicking, wondering where I was.

I turned the corner happily and someone suddenly grabbed my hand and went, "There you are!" in an out-of-breath voice.

I turned to find myself staring into the familiar dark brown eyes of Connor Lawrence.

And in that moment I felt a strange calm for the first time in weeks because I suddenly realized what I had to do.

26.

CONNOR LOOKED LIKE A MOVIE STAR. HE WAS wearing a pale gray suit and a narrow black tie, and his bangs were slickly swept back, instead of flopping over his eyes the whole time.

His brown eyes looked even more intense than usual now that they weren't hidden away.

"Wow, Connor," I said, unashamedly looking him up and down. "You look *great*."

"Thanks." He smiled nervously. "My mom figured that if I was ever going to make an effort with my appearance, it should probably be today. You look great too. Nice, er, dress?"

"Yes, I suspect lots of people will be trying to decide whether I have, in fact, turned up at my father's wedding wearing a giant macaroon." I laughed. "I'm glad you made it here okay. I can't believe that Dad and Helena changed everything and I didn't have any clue! You did very well keeping it a secret when I was saying all that stuff in your room yesterday about Dad."

"It was hard, believe me. You were so worried. Your mom told me the other day as soon as we got in the car, just after you invited me." He raised his eyebrows. "So how come you're out in the courtyard on your own? Marianne said you just ran out of the room in a panic. That terrifying wedding woman is having a heart attack in there."

"Oh. I wanted to . . ." I thought about lying, but then I figured that it was way more effort than it was worth. And if anyone was going to get this, it would be Connor. "I actually wanted to talk to Dad. I wanted to make sure he was okay with what lies in store after today. Basically, what you warned me about."

He nodded. "Everything good?"

"Yes. And that actually brings me onto something else. Connor, I need to talk to you about—"

"ANNA!" Fenella's shrill cry made me jump in fright. "You can't just run off like that! Where have you been?"

She stormed toward me, grabbed my arm, and yanked me back inside.

"I . . . uh . . . I . . ." I quickly tried to think of an excuse as we came into the reception area and Marianne turned around, sighing with relief and looking daggers at me.

"She was looking for me," Connor said, stepping forward. "I forgot to tell her that I was going to meet her in here instead. We had arranged to meet in the courtyard originally and then I changed my plan. My fault."

Fenella narrowed her eyes at him. "Thankfully, it hasn't disrupted the schedule. Helena will be down any moment and the guests are all seated. Anna, this young man will be walking you down the aisle. I hope his walking is better than his lying."

She turned on her heel and marched toward the wedding team, barking instructions at them and ensuring all their headsets were working.

"I'm glad you're here, Connor," Marianne said, looking through the now empty reception area and toward the doors to the hall where the ceremony was being held. "Someone has to make sure Anna doesn't fall over."

"Hey! I haven't fallen over once today!"

"Would you like a medal?"

I opened my mouth to argue but there was a ripple of gasps from the wedding team. I turned just in time to see Helena glide elegantly down the stairs, holding her blossoming bouquet of summer flowers in one hand and gently lifting her dress so it was just off the ground with the other.

"What do you think?" she asked nervously, glancing from Marianne to me.

"Helena." I smiled. "For a guy who has written the most boring book in the world on tanks, my dad has done VERY well."

She started laughing and Marianne wiped a tear from her cheek. "You look beautiful, Mom," she whispered. "I would come and hug you, but I don't think I can in this dress."

"And I haven't scheduled in time for hugs," Fenella added, tapping her watch. "They're waiting in there for me to give the signal. I'll go tell them now, and then the doors will be opened for you from the inside. Anna and Connor, you walk down first, Marianne to follow, and then the bride." She took a long, deep breath and then went, "It's time," in a dramatically hushed voice.

She blew a kiss at Helena and then scurried down the corridor where there must have been a side door leading to the main hall, while the rest of the wedding team, still lurking, led the way to the doors, getting us into position and then stepping aside. Connor and I stood next to each other at the front, waiting in silence for it all to begin.

"So what was it that you wanted to talk to me about outside?" he asked softly.

"It can wait." I took a deep, shaky breath. "I really, really hope I don't fall over."

"You won't," Connor whispered. "Just lean on me."

He held out his arm, I took it, and the doors swung open.

"You look wonderful!" my mom said, stretching over my dress to squeeze my cheek after the ceremony was done. I had finished having my photo taken with the bride and groom and had eventually located Connor, backed into a corner away from the crowd. Mom had come over to join us, her eyes glistening with tears.

"It was just magical, wasn't it?" Mom said to Connor, who nodded politely. "Just like a dream."

As embarrassing as she sounded, Mom was right—it really was a very beautiful wedding. Fenella had created a stunning spectacle.

When the doors had opened, I thought my eyes might pop out as we stepped onto what looked like a very expensive

Hollywood movie set for a production of A *Midsummer Night's Dream*. There were candles everywhere around the room, and hundreds and hundreds of white flowers, not just adorning the chairs on which the guests were perched, but tumbling down the walls so that it would have been easy to forget that you were even indoors.

There was a harpist playing as we came down the aisle, and Dad, standing by the altar, gave me such a big smile when I tottered toward him—concentrating very hard on not knocking over chairs and candlesticks with my dress—that I actually welled up.

By the time they said "I do" I was practically sobbing.

Luckily, the netting on my dress doubled perfectly as a tissue, although I don't think Fenella was all that impressed when she saw me dabbing at my face with my skirt in the front row.

"Weddings are always fun." Connor smiled after my mom had finished telling him the story about the Indian wedding she attended when an elephant stepped on the train of her sari dress and almost unraveled it, which would have left her naked in front of everyone.

Thankfully, just at that moment, one of her friends came over to greet her, and Connor was rescued from any more traumatizing stories.

"Want to get out of here?" Connor suggested as he dodged a silver tray of champagne flutes that a waiter was carrying past.

"Sure." I glanced at Fenella, who was busy accepting compliments from the hotel manager. "We have a bit of time now before the meal."

He led the way through the crowd and out into the open air, with me trailing behind, parting the masses with my dress.

"Phew!" I said, finally breaking through. "It is busy in there!"

"Anna, I know what you wanted to talk to me about earlier," he admitted with a grave expression.

"You do?"

"Yeah." He hesitated, shuffling his feet, and then he lifted his eyes to meet mine. "It's not right, is it? With us. Right now. Something's not right."

"No," I said, a lump forming in my throat, thinking of how obviously perfect my dad and Helena had been just now. "It's not."

"The truth is, Anna, you happen to be the coolest girl I ever met. But you also now happen to be . . ." He trailed off and looked back down at the floor.

I knew what he was going to say so I finished the sentence for him. I think I had known all along.

"An It Girl?"

"Yes, but it's not just that. I always knew that was going to happen. We've both changed, I think. We're not bad different—just different . . ." He searched for the words.

"It's okay," I said gently. And I meant it. Connor was right. "Anyway, you have to focus on your comic book now."

He nodded slowly. "I think, if you don't mind, I'll head home and give it some finishing touches."

"Now? Really?" I glanced back at all the guests chatting loudly. When I turned back, he was watching me closely. "You're going to miss the reception?"

"I thought it might be a good idea if I bowed out quietly."

The chatting behind us ceased as Fenella's booming voice invited the guests to move into the dining room and take their seats.

"You better go," he said. "If that was just the ceremony, I'd say you were in for an amazing evening."

"Right." I nodded, not really knowing what to do.

He leaned over my massive dress and gave me the gentlest of kisses on the cheek.

Then he pulled away from me, shoved his hands in his pockets, and started to walk down the steps.

"Connor," I called. He stopped and looked back. "Thanks for being here today."

He smiled at me with that mischievous smile he used to shoot me when we sat in detention together. "Always, Spidey."

Then he turned away and walked down the remaining steps, around the corner, and out of sight.

27.

NORMAL WEDDING VS. HUNTLEY/MONTAINE WEDDING

1. At a normal wedding, the bride and groom enter the reception after the ceremony, and everyone stands and applauds as they take their seats at the head table. *At a Huntley/Montaine wedding, the bride and groom enter the reception ACCOMPANIED BY A HAREM OF PEACOCKS.*

2. At a normal wedding, before the meal begins, there is polite chatter as everyone gets to know the fellow guests on their table. *At a Huntley/ Montaine wedding, before the meal begins, a troop of totally random acrobats enters the room and performs a routine on top of the tables, which involves fire, swords, and a nineties pop soundtrack.*

3. At a normal wedding, the meal is typically a lovely three-course meal often involving chicken. *At a Huntley/Montaine wedding, the meal is cooked by a Michelin-starred celebrity chef who has decided to surprise the bride and groom by wheeling out a large silver platter on which he has created a life-size portrait of the happy couple using tomatoes, mango chutney, olives, and coriander.*

4. At a normal wedding, the speeches finish with a roar of laughter, a round of applause, and a joyful toast. *At a Huntley/Montaine wedding, the speeches finish with a roar of laughter, a round of applause, a joyful toast, AND glitter and confetti bursting from the ceiling as a large choir bursts through the doors singing "Don't Stop Me Now" by Queen, accompanied by the Royal Philharmonic Orchestra.*

5. At a normal wedding, the band or DJ begins to play, the bride and groom have their first dance, and then the guests are invited to join them on the dance floor. *At a Huntley/Montaine wedding, Elton John gets up onstage to sing*

the first romantic dance number, and then is joined by the biggest boy band in the world, which causes all the guests to lose their minds and run onto the dance floor screaming, while the groom gets out of there as quickly as possible, goes over to his daughter, and says, "Who are these punks again? Should I have heard of them?" before he kindly asks a waiter for an Irish whiskey and then goes to discuss politics with the prime minister of Sweden.

"This wedding is surely going to go down in history," Marianne said before a fresh bout of screams exploded from the dance floor when the boy band launched into their latest number one single.

We had both moved back to our seats at the head table after watching Helena and my dad waltz around the floor for their first dance. (Which, by the way, was hilarious. He should have gotten lessons. The prima ballerina of the Royal Ballet, who happened to be standing next to me at the time, wholeheartedly agreed.)

I hadn't thought it possible, but the reception was even more glamorous than the ceremony. The vast ceiling was dark blue and completely covered in hundreds of twinkling lights, so it looked *exactly* like clusters of stars in a night sky.

"It really is quite something," I replied, picking at the chocolate mousse left on my plate. "Although, what was with the peacocks?"

"What was with the tomato portrait?" Marianne laughed. "Bonkers!"

"Well, suits our parents completely, then."

"That's true." She sighed and poured herself a glass of water. "So are you ever going to tell me why you asked Fenella in a very panicked manner to clear Connor's space at the table and move everyone up a place before the dinner began? Or can I guess?"

My cheeks went piping hot. "You can guess?"

"I think so. Did you guys break up?" she asked gently.

I nodded. "How did you know?"

"I had my suspicions. What happened? Are you okay?"

I shrugged. "I guess so. I want to blame it on the whole fame thing but I think it's just as much me as that. I've accepted being an It Girl over the last year and all the craziness that comes with it—and changed because of it. But I don't think Connor has. And that's not a bad thing—it's just not a Me thing anymore. Does that make sense?"

"It does. I actually had a feeling something was not quite right with you guys before you went away," Marianne admitted.

"Really? How? And why didn't you tell me?"

"Because I didn't want to upset you! And I wasn't sure. Just the way you were together—there was something restrained about it. You just didn't light up anymore the way you do when you're talking about Rome, for example . . ." She sighed. "If only I had seen things with me and He Who Must Not Be Named so clearly!"

My mouth dropped open.

"Why are you looking at me weirdly like that?" she asked.

"Because of the Harry Potter reference!" I cried, gripping her arm. "You really are a nerd just like me! I didn't even know you liked the books! We should totally do a film marathon of the whole series!"

"What Harry Potter reference?" She looked mildly disturbed at my enthusiasm. "I was talking about Tom."

"Oh. Never mind."

Marianne became distracted with attempting to flatten the bouffant-shaped sleeves of her dress. "Well, I hope you're okay with the whole breakup thing. I'm sorry that it happened at the wedding, but at least you know it was the right thing to do."

"Geez, I feel now that everyone was kind of hinting at this. Dad asked me about my love life earlier, which was way out of character—and embarrassing—and in Rome, Sophie even hinted at it, which is annoyingly observant of her and I—" I stopped and sat bolt upright.

"What? Why are you making that face?" Marianne looked at me in worry. "Anna, you've gone pale! What's wrong?"

"Sophie," I whispered.

"What about her?"

"She's meant to be coming to the wedding." I gulped, reaching for Marianne's hand. "I promised her she could come if she helped me sneak out of the hotel in Rome. She's going to kill me when she finds out the wedding has been and gone!"

"Oh, that." Marianne checked the gold clock that was hanging above the large doors to the room. "You just reminded me. I told them to get here around now."

"Who? Wait. You told Sophie? How did you know to tell her?"

"The message got passed on by some other guests you might be happy to see." She nodded toward something behind me. "Perfect timing."

I turned to see the doors being opened, and to my

complete surprise, Jess, Danny, and Stephanie sheepishly shuffled into the room, looking immediately dumbfounded by the scene before them. I screamed in joy and jumped up, rushing toward them and sweeping them all up for a big hug, laughing as they became caught up in the ruffles of my dress.

Danny was wearing a tuxedo with a bright blue bow tie and had somehow managed to tame his bouncy, blond curls in such a way that I had to admit looked very handsome. Stephanie looked very elegant next to him in a long pale blue dress, almost matching his bow tie, and she had done her hair up in curls on top of her head with her bangs pinned back.

But Jess had really gone to town. The last time I'd seen her dress smartly was at the Beatus dance in the second semester when she'd worn a very pretty short black dress, but this time she had gone all out. She looked like a supermodel in what can only be described as a GOWN.

Yes, Jess, the girl who wears a hundred different colors on her nails at once, dip-dyes her hair, and is rarely out of her gym uniform, was wearing a gown. Not just any gown either. It was a striking dark turquoise, strapless, and full length, floating out as it draped to the bottom of her endless legs. Her diamond earrings glittered underneath her professionally curled hair, falling in waves across her shoulders.

If I hadn't pounced on her straightaway, I'm certain that almost every boy in the room would have done.

"I feel like I've been swallowed by a marshmallow!" she gasped as I hugged her.

"Oh my," Stephanie gushed. "I can't believe I'm actually here! This is incredible."

"Now that you're all here, my night has gotten WAY better!" I exclaimed, shaking Jess's hand excitedly.

I had been kind of worried about bringing out The Octopus dance move, you know, in front of a bunch of celebrities and global royalty, but now that my friends were present I started to do some arm stretches in preparation.

"You might not think that when you see what else we've got in store for you," Jess grimaced, turning to face the door, which opened right on cue to reveal none other than Sophie Parker.

"You did promise her." Danny laughed, as we watched her stride in confidently and make a beeline for the dance floor. "She made quite a fuss with the security, asking them to take photos with some of the celebrities hanging around outside."

"I can imagine." I laughed.

Sophie swept her gaze across the room and stopped when she spotted me. She lifted her hand and waved with a smile. A SMILE.

And, okay, it was the smallest smile of all time and looked as though it were a HUGE amount of effort for her to contort her face into a smiling position but it was 100 percent a smile.

You know what that means? I was right. In Rome, we *totally* bonded.

Marianne came over to join us, hugging the new arrivals each in turn and then throwing an arm around me. "Good surprise?"

"The best!"

"Helena and Dad thought it would be nice if you could have your all your friends here," Marianne explained.

I searched the room for Dad and saw him watching me. My eyes filled with tears at how thoughtful he had been. He held up his glass in acknowledgement and then went back to his conversation.

"He also thought your best friend should be here." Marianne grinned. "I'll go explain to security that he can come in."

She tottered off, exiting through the door, leaving me totally confused. "Who is she talking about?"

"Wait and see," Stephanie squealed excitedly.

"More surprises?" I shook my head in astonishment. "Dad really has been busy. I feel bad now for making fun of his hair the past few weeks."

Desperately trying to work out who could possibly arrive next—reminding myself that the likelihood of comic-book god Stan Lee turning up was very slight since, unfortunately, I don't think Dad even knows who he is—I waited impatiently for the doors to open again.

When they finally did, at first it didn't look like anyone was there and it was just opening for no reason. But then I lowered my gaze.

"DOG!" I cried, as he trotted in wearing a top hat and bow tie.

I think I scared him a little bit at first in my dress, but when he realized that he wasn't being attacked by some kind of giant purple alien he perked up, leaping to try and lick my face.

I complimented him on his smart attire—that, Marianne informed me, was my mom's doing and not Dad's— before Dog got bored of me fussing over him and started sniffing around the floor for some Michelin-starred scraps.

I straightened up, grinning so wide that my jaw ached, and that's when I saw the person who had brought Dog.

I didn't even care that all my friends were watching. I didn't even care if my dad, my mom, and a whole lot of celebrities and members of the royal family were watching. And I certainly didn't care that Sophie Parker was watching.

I rushed toward James and into his arms, the weight of my lilac bridesmaid's monstrosity knocking him clean off his feet so we landed in a heap on the floor. "Good to see you, too." He laughed, pushing the frills away from his face so he could see mine. I beamed at him.

It's like Dad said. Sometimes, you just know.

28.

"SO?" JESS SAID, SLUMPING DOWN ONTO THE SOFA
with a bowl of popcorn. "What was it like?"

Dog had been lying comfortably on his back with his four
paws sticking up in the air, but as soon as the smell of warm,
salty popcorn drifted in the room, he was up like a shot, racing
over to her. She batted away his snout.

"What do you mean?" I laughed, sitting next to her.

"Duh!" Marianne picked up the cushion from the chair
she was slouched in and threw it at me. "The kissing! Don't
think I didn't see him give you a sneaky smooch on the dance
floor."

"It was good." I blushed, refusing to look at either of them
and instead studying the embroidery of the cushion I had
caught.

"It was hilarious the way you knocked him over when he
walked through the door." Jess shook her head. "It was literally

like a giant purple snowball flying through the air."

"You guys make a great couple," Marianne added, smiling at me.

"Agreed," Jess said, before narrowing her eyes at my Labrador, who was still watching the bowl of popcorn intensely. "Ew! Dog, stop drooling on my leg!"

"I've known for ages you and James were going to end up together," Marianne informed us smugly.

"How?" I said, wishing my cheeks would stop burning. "*I* didn't even know it was going to happen."

"Well, the way you talked about him was all"—she wrinkled her nose—"gooey."

"It was not!" I shrieked, throwing the cushion back at her.

"It was!" She laughed, wiggling her feet in her Winnie-the-Pooh slippers. "Ever since you came back from Rome. Plus there was that photo you showed me."

"What photo?"

"When you were showing me Jess's pictures from the vacation. The one of you and James standing next to some kind of gargoyle thing . . ."

"I know the one," Jess said. "When Anna was giving us a boring lecture about some old film and that ugly stone dude eats your hand or something."

"The *Bocca della Verità*." I blushed, remembering James's hand next to mine.

"It was the perfect moment," Jess said proudly. "Completely natural, I caught them unaware."

"They say a picture tells a thousand words. . . ." Marianne and Jess looked at each other knowingly.

"I'm surprised it took you so long to realize." Jess threw a kernel of popcorn in the air and it dropped into her mouth. "It was so obvious all last semester that he was crazy about you. And every time he walks in the room your face lights up."

"You never said anything before now!"

"Had to let you work it out for yourself. Would have given away all the fun. You two are adorable."

"All right," I sighed. "We can talk about something else now."

"Making you embarrassed, are we? You didn't seem too embarrassed last night when you were slow dancing together the whole time." Jess winked at me.

"I wasn't the only one! What about you slow dancing with that guy from the orchestra?"

"Oh, please," Jess snorted. "It is so NOT about musicians."

Marianne nodded. "I hear that." They high-fived each other and I rolled my eyes.

"No spark, then?"

"I'm only interested in Italian men these days," Jess stated, making me giggle. "I've been messaging a certain sound guy . . ."

"What? The one in Rome?"

"He wants to practice his written English," Jess said smugly. "I selflessly offered my services. We're pen pals, if you will. For now. I just need to apply for Italian photography courses."

I glanced over at Marianne, who was typing into her phone. "And what about you, Marianne?"

"What about me?"

"You were talking to that tall bearded dude for ages," I said. "What was all that about?"

"That 'tall bearded dude' happens to work at one of the top British fashion labels. We were having a business conversation. He wants to work with me in the future," she said coyly.

"Work with you how?" Jess asked excitedly.

"Well, he mentioned my own clothing line. . . ."

I shrieked, jumped off the sofa, and went to sit on top of her to give her a hug. "That is SO cool!"

"Oof! Anna!" Marianne yelped as I landed on her and smothered her with my Snoopy nightgown. "It's still early days!"

"What did he say?"

"He said that if I managed to make that ridiculous bridesmaid dress look fashionable then he thought I had excellent potential." Marianne laughed.

"I think that's brilliant!"

"I think what was more brilliant was you helping Sophie out," Marianne chuckled. "Don't think we didn't see that."

"Ah, yes, that."

When I saw Sophie standing all alone to the side of the dance floor, craning her neck, desperately trying to spot a celebrity she might be able to talk to, I genuinely felt sorry for her.

"You felt sorry for Sophie Parker?" Jess snorted. "That's a first."

But I really did feel bad for her, especially as we were all having so much fun and she was just stuck there on her own. So I walked over to where Sophie was standing.

"Hey."

"Hey," she said, eyeing me up and down. "That dress is awful."

"I know."

"It's a nice wedding."

"Yeah, it's cool."

"Thanks," she said hurriedly, clearly not wanting to dwell

on this necessary point of the conversation, "for letting me come."

"I said I would. Anyway, let me introduce you to someone," I offered, grabbing her arm and steering her around the dance floor.

I tapped the shoulder of one of the members of the boy band who were taking a break from their set. He didn't seem to mind being disturbed when I introduced Sophie to him, and soon she was deep in conversation with him about their latest tour that she had bought tickets to. She was so enamored by him that I didn't think she would notice me slink off, but just as I backed away she grabbed my arm.

"Thanks, Anna," she said quietly. "Again."

"Is this bonding?"

"Seriously, Anna. You ruin it every time. No, we are not."

But I'm sure I caught a smile as I slunk away.

"Sophie will be busy telling everyone she knows that she spent the whole night with a famous boy band," Jess moaned. "We'll never hear the end of it. But, anyway, my highlight was when Dog crashed into that table and knocked over the wedding cake." She threw some popcorn up in the air for Dog to catch.

He missed and it stuck to his nose, making us all burst out laughing.

"I thought Mom and Nick reacted to him destroying their four-tiered, bespoke wedding cake fairly well." Marianne chuckled as Dog finally managed to scoop the popcorn from his nose with his tongue and munch away happily.

"Yeah. Dad just said it wasn't like it was the biggest day of his life and the cake cost more than our house or anything." I grinned, reaching across to Dog to tickle his chin. "I thought it was game over for Dad's eyebrows."

"It wouldn't have been right if Dog hadn't made his mark. Nick was adamant that he should be there," Marianne informed me.

"Dad is *definitely* going soft in his old age," I remarked.

"They should be back any minute from breakfast," Marianne said, looking at her watch. "So nice of Rebecca to organize that as a surprise wedding present. Mom loves that restaurant."

Marianne heaved herself up from the chair. "I better head off. I'm meeting a friend. Dog, go fetch my shoes! Go on! Go fetch!" Marianne pointed at the door and Dog tottered out. She kicked off her slippers and raised her eyebrows at Jess and me snickering together on the sofa. "What's so funny?"

"Have you met Dog?" Jess laughed.

"Now that you're one of the family, you need to learn that

Dog is an independent soul and will work on his own terms," I advised.

"Is that so?" Marianne said.

"I can't believe you expect Dog to know which are your shoes and just bring them along to you!" Jess wheezed.

The door pushed open and Dog walked in carrying a pair of bright blue strapped heels, which he placed obediently at Marianne's dainty feet before he sat down next to her with his chin up and tongue lolling out, waiting for the praise that she duly began to give him.

Jess and I stared at Dog with our mouths hanging open.

"Well, what do you know?" Marianne said, sliding on her shoes, grabbing her bag, and heading out.

She closed the door behind her, and Jess and I didn't move, silenced by the miracle that had just happened before our eyes.

"Dog?" I said, scrutinizing his face as he padded over to me. "Is that really you?"

He tilted his head and then suddenly launched himself forward onto the sofa with us, winding and headbutting me at the same time.

"Dog!" I groaned, rubbing my forehead. He licked my nose and then decided to settle down and curl up on my lap, forgetting he was a gigantic Labrador.

"It just goes to show." Jess laughed. "You may be a celebrity these days with a Hollywood movie star stepmom and the coolest socialite stepsister of all time, but when it comes down to it you're just as much of a loser as you always were."

"Yeah." I smiled as Jess let out another yawn, wiggled across the sofa with the popcorn, and rested her head on my shoulder. "Some things never change."

29.

From: rebecca.blythe@bounce-mail.co.uk
To: anna_huntley@zingmail.co.uk
Subject: A perfect wedding!

Well, I have to say that was the best evening
I have had in a long time! Such a wonderful
wedding. I hope you enjoyed it, darling. At
the last wedding I took you to, you jumped
into the aisle in the middle of the marriage
vows, bent over so your bottom was in the air
pointing at all the guests, and shouted "BUM
BUM!" at the top of your lungs. Boy, did that
church echo.

So I was relieved that you behaved impeccably
at this one. Well done!

I'm very much looking forward to coming to
house-sit and spending two weeks with you

while your father and Helena jet off on their
honeymoon. I know they'll be running around
like headless chickens after they get back from
breakfast, sorting everything before they go,
but I will be arriving this afternoon to help
pack them into the taxi.
See you soon, darling!
Mom xxx

PS Such a shame that Marianne's rice trick
didn't save your cell phone! Now that the
chaos of the wedding is over, I think it's about
time we got you a new one, don't you?

From: anna_huntley@zingmail.co.uk
To: rebecca.blythe@bounce-mail.co.uk
Subject: Re: A perfect wedding!
NEVER TELL ANYONE THE BUM BUM
STORY.
Please confirm receipt of this e-mail.

From: rebecca.blythe@bounce-mail.co.uk
To: anna_huntley@zingmail.co.uk

Subject: Re: A perfect wedding!
If you like, darling!
I certainly won't tell anyone the Bum Bum
story. From now.
Mom xxx

From: anna_huntley@zingmail.co.uk
To: rebecca.blythe@bounce-mail.co.uk
Subject: Re: A perfect wedding!
What do you mean "from now"?

From: rebecca.blythe@bounce-mail.co.uk
To: anna_huntley@zingmail.co.uk
Subject: Re: A perfect wedding!
By the way, what would you like for your
birthday this year? I can't believe you're turning
fifteen in just over a week!
How about that new cell phone? Let's go
shopping for it. That will be so much fun!
Mom xxx

From: anna_huntley@zingmail.co.uk
To: rebecca.blythe@bounce-mail.co.uk

Subject: Re: A perfect wedding!
WHAT DO YOU MEAN "FROM NOW"?

From: rebecca.blythe@bounce-mail.co.uk
To: anna_huntley@zingmail.co.uk
Subject: Re: A perfect wedding!
Don't panic, Anna. It may have slipped out last
night at the wedding. You know how it is, small
talk with the other guests.
It seemed like an appropriate story to tell,
considering the setting.
And everyone found it hilarious! If anything,
you'll be much more popular now.
Mom xxx

From: anna_huntley@zingmail.co.uk
To: rebecca.blythe@bounce-mail.co.uk
Subject: Re: A perfect wedding!
Brilliant, thanks, Mom.
PS My life is over.

From: anna_huntley@zingmail.co.uk
To: jess.delby@zingmail.co.uk

Cc: dantheman@zingmail.co.uk
Subject: Well hello there
Hey! Looking forward to seeing you both in a bit for pizza.
Just out of interest, neither of you talked to my mom at the wedding, did you? You didn't chat with her, right?
You didn't mention anything this morning, Jess, so guessing you both managed to avoid her?
Love, me xxx

From: dantheman@zingmail.co.uk
To: jess.delby@zingmail.co.uk
Cc: anna_huntley@zingmail.co.uk
Subject: Re: Well hello there
No, I don't recall that we did. Why?
Danny

From: anna_huntley@zingmail.co.uk
To: jess.delby@zingmail.co.uk
Cc: dantheman@zingmail.co.uk

Subject: Re: Well hello there
Oh good. No reason! See you later.
Love, me xxx

From: jess.delby@zingmail.co.uk
To: anna_huntley@zingmail.co.uk
Cc: dantheman@zingmail.co.uk
Subject: Re: Well hello there
By the way, I meant to say before I left this
morning, well done on not shouting "BUM
BUM" at any point during the wedding.
A real achievement.
J x

From: dantheman@zingmail.co.uk
To: jess.delby@zingmail.co.uk
Cc: anna_huntley@zingmail.co.uk
Subject: Re: Well hello there
Yeah, if you'd done that Anna, you would have
really hit rock BOTTOM.
Ha.
Danny

From: jess.delby@zingmail.co.uk
To: dantheman@zingmail.co.uk
Cc: anna_huntley@zingmail.co.uk
Subject: Haha
We mean this from the BOTTOM of our hearts.
J x

From: dantheman@zingmail.co.uk
To: jess.delby@zingmail.co.uk
Cc: anna_huntley@zingmail.co.uk
Subject: Re: Haha
And that is the BOTTOM line.
Danny

From: jess.delby@zingmail.co.uk
To: dantheman@zingmail.co.uk
Cc: anna_huntley@zingmail.co.uk
Subject: Re: Haha
I'm glad you're not BUM-med out about it.
J x

From: dantheman@zingmail.co.uk
To: jess.delby@zingmail.co.uk

Cc: anna_huntley@zingmail.co.uk
Subject: Re: Haha
I'm going to go have a drink. BOTTOMs up!
Danny

From: anna_huntley@zingmail.co.uk
To: dantheman@zingmail.co.uk
Cc: jess.delby@zingmail.co.uk
Subject: Re: Haha
ALL RIGHT, YOU'VE HAD YOUR FUN.
I'm going to spend the rest of the summer in
the broom closet and never talk to you two
ever again.
Good day to you!
Love, me xxx

PS I was VERY little when the bum-bum
incident occurred.
PPS What time are you both coming over?
Jess, since you left I've been teaching myself a
new speech from *Lord of the Rings* and I want
to try it out on you guys.
PPPS Dog is playing the part of Aragorn.

From: tyndale@bounce-mail.co.uk
To: anna_huntley@zingmail.co.uk
Subject: Quick note

Hey Anna,

I know we spoke on the phone just now but
I forgot to ask . . . were you being serious
yesterday when you said that you owned a Star
Wars lightsaber?

I thought that came up in conversation last
night but I may have made it up.

James xxx

From: anna_huntley@zingmail.co.uk
To: tyndale@bounce-mail.co.uk
Subject: Re: Quick note

Of course I don't own a lightsaber!

Who do you think I am? Some kind of
nerd?

xxx

From: tyndale@bounce-mail.co.uk
To: anna_huntley@zingmail.co.uk
Subject: Re: Quick note

You do, don't you.

xxx

From: anna_huntley@zingmail.co.uk
To: tyndale@bounce-mail.co.uk
Subject: Re: Quick note
Maybe.

xxx

From: tyndale@bounce-mail.co.uk
To: anna_huntley@zingmail.co.uk
Subject: Re: Quick note
Just so you know, I intend to tease you about
this for the rest of time.

xxx

PS Excited to see you next week.

From: anna_huntley@zingmail.co.uk
To: tyndale@bounce-mail.co.uk
Subject: Re: Quick note
In which case, I will be teasing you for the rest
of time about how you know all the words to

"Girls Just Wanna Have Fun."
Don't deny it. I saw you singing along last night, Tyndale.

xxx

PS Me too.
PPS I'll buy you a lightsaber too and we can fight!!

From: anna_huntley@zingmail.co.uk
To: tyndale@bounce-mail.co.uk
Subject: DON'T READ PREVIOUS E-MAIL MESSAGE

I would appreciate it if you could ignore that last PPS.
I just read it back and it sounds ridiculous.

xxx

From: tyndale@bounce-mail.co.uk
To: anna_huntley@zingmail.co.uk
Subject: Re: DON'T READ PREVIOUS E-MAIL MESSAGE

I've printed it out to get it framed.

xxx

PS I already ordered a lightsaber online. Keep up, nerd.

From: anna_huntley@zingmail.co.uk
To: marianne@montaines.co.uk
Subject: Hey, sister!
Look, are you coming over soon?
Dad keeps telling me I look adorable in my
Snoopy nightgown.
It's freaking me out.

From: marianne@montaines.co.uk
To: anna_huntley@zingmail.co.uk
Subject: Re: Hey, sister!
I'm setting off in a few minutes.
It's because he just got married and he's off on
his honeymoon. He's ridiculously happy. Leave
him alone.
Marianne x

From: anna_huntley@zingmail.co.uk
To: marianne@montaines.co.uk
Subject: Re: Hey, sister!
I just sprayed him in the face with my water gun hoping to wake him from this dazed state and do you know what he did?
His eyebrows barely flinched and he laughed. HE LAUGHED.
I think you may be right. He really is happy. Weird.

From: marianne@montaines.co.uk
To: anna_huntley@zingmail.co.uk
Subject: Re: Hey, sister!
Well then, this is all brilliant evidence to present to Sophie next term.
We're getting our happy ending after all.
M x

PS Am about to make my way through a horde of paparazzi. Have taken inspiration from your last e-mail. Am armed with a water gun. This should be good.

From: anna_huntley@zingmail.co.uk

To: marianne@montaines.co.uk

Subject: Re: Hey, sister!

Who said anything about an ending?

xxx

PS See you on the other side.

ACKNOWLEDGMENTS

A massive thank you to Lindsey Heaven, Lauren Clarke, Jo Hayes, Alice Hill, and the incredible teams at Egmont and Bell Lomax Moreton. Thanks to you, Anna's story came alive and this writer's dream came true. I will always be grateful to you for believing in Anna.

Big, big thank you to my amazing friends for the support, encouragement and all the laughs. You might have noticed a strong theme of friendship running through this series. That's down to you lot. Thank you for the never-ending inspiration.

A very special thank you to my wonderful family for always being there cheering me on—you truly are the best family anyone could ever wish for and I will always look up to you.

My beautiful godson and nephew, Sam—your little smile got me through some pretty serious writer's block. I can't wait until you start reading and we can read together.

ACKNOWLEDGMENTS

The character of Dog was created thanks to the combined genius of Badger, Amber, Dougal, Archie, and Lara Birchall. Loyal companions, keepers of secrets, true friends. If you have a dog, you'll know what I mean.

Lastly, thank you to anyone who reads this book. I hope it makes you smile.

I SET JOSIE GRAHAM ON FIRE.

And, okay, yes it was bad, but it was an accident and not *entirely* my fault. Everyone thinks I did it on purpose. They think Mrs. Ginnwell is a hero.

If you ask me, Mrs. Ginnwell made the whole thing worse. A little bit of water would have sorted everything out just fine. It was only the ends of her hair, and a fire extinguisher was a very dramatic plan of action. I mean, Josie was already having a pretty bad day considering I'd just set her on fire and everything, and the next thing she knew she was covered head to toe in that white foamy stuff that always looks like it might be fun to play in but probably isn't. (I think Josie looked more in shock—and a little bit itchy—than like she was having fun.)

I was kind of in shock myself. I'd never set fire to anyone before so the whole incident came as a bit of a surprise. The closest I've been to any kind of arson was when I was little and I put my dad's wallet on the fire log to see what would happen. I mean, who leaves their wallet lying around in the same room as a toddler? Not my father anymore that's for sure. But I still think he looks at me a little bit suspiciously on cold nights.

Oh, and there *was* that time I almost burned down Dad's study. But those two times are IT.

And you know what? This is partly Josie Graham's fault too. Because really, she should not have been (a) leaning on her hand so close to a Bunsen burner and (b) wearing so much hairspray to school.

I'm just jealous because I don't have the time, let alone the skills, for hairspray. Once Dad has eventually wrestled the duvet cover away from me, I have about ten minutes tops to get ready.

My dad would never buy me hairspray anyway. He's so old-fashioned, especially when it comes to his twelve-year-old daughter. I remember one time in a drugstore I asked him if he would buy me eyeliner. He burst out laughing and made me go fetch some Theraflu. I think this is VERY hypocritical as some of the women my dad has dated have worn a LOT of dark eyeliner. How would he feel if, when he introduced them, I laughed in their face and gave them a mug of hot lemon acetaminophen instead?

Hmm . . . I might consider this for the really annoying ones that get brought home.

A wobbling Mrs. Ginnwell definitely wasn't laughing as she marched me into Ms. Duke's office mumbling something incoherent about fire in the classroom and pyromaniac tendencies.

"Sorry, Mrs. Ginnwell, I didn't quite understand that. What did you say?" Ms. Duke asked, rising from her desk with a look of concern.

Ms. Duke really suits her office. Which sounds strange when I say it out loud, but it just goes with her overall vibe. She's new to the school too. We were both new in September, although obviously she's a bit more senior being principal and everything. I just started seventh grade. Everything considered, I think she has managed to set the better impression out of the two of us so far. This is not great seeing as she gives out detentions and makes people pick up trash from behind the bike rack.

So even though she's only been in that office for a semester and I'm not entirely sure what it looked like before she arrived, it matches her. For example, it's all very neat. Ms. Duke is very formal and smartly dressed. She looks more like those businesswomen who are always on their hands-free cell phones in train stations barking things like, "That's just not good enough, Jeffrey," than a principal at a co-ed school.

I like the way she can pull off a pantsuit though. I think if ever I was going to work in an office I would like to wear a pantsuit and look authoritative like Ms. Duke does. And her dark hair is always so neatly pinned and her makeup never smudged. She is very intimidating.

Even more so when you've just set your classmate's hair on fire.

"Chemistry class . . . Anna . . . Anna set . . . hair . . . Josie Graham on fire!" Mrs. Ginnwell finally spluttered.

Mrs. Ginnwell is neither authoritative nor intimidating. She kind of reminds me of a parrot. But not a cool one that would chill with a pirate. An overzealous one that swoops around your head, squawking and whacking you unexpectedly in the face with its wings.

"Is Josie all right?" Ms. Duke asked in alarm.

Mrs. Ginnwell nodded, her curled strawberry-blond hair frizzing around her sweaty forehead. "Fine. Although her hair is quite singed and covered in foam."

"I see," Ms. Duke replied, and I swear I saw her smirk for

a second. If she did, it was gone in an instant when she caught my eye. "And no one else was hurt in this incident?"

"No." Mrs. Ginnwell shook her head.

"Well in that case, Anna, you can have a seat and, Jenny, why don't you pop into the teachers' lounge and ask someone to cover your lesson for a bit while you get a cup of coffee."

Mrs. Ginnwell nodded and slowly released her grip on me. She gave me a very pointed look, as if when let loose I would pull out a flamethrower from my locker and burn the school to the ground. Which is a completely ridiculous thought for her to entertain because last semester I did an excellent essay on penguins. No one who puts that much effort and emotional maturity into a seventh-grade essay about penguins would be spending their free time plotting to destroy their school.

I sat down slowly into the leather chair opposite Ms. Duke, who was settling into her chair behind the desk. The heavy wooden door closed loudly as Mrs. Ginnwell escaped, still glaring at me, and there was a moment of silence as Ms. Duke straightened the forms she had been filling in before we interrupted her afternoon.

"So, why don't you explain to me exactly what happened?"

I took a deep breath and told her how we had been in our chemistry class and Josie and I had been partnered together, which, by the way, neither of us were too happy about. I didn't tell Ms. Duke that part though.

I assumed she would know that it had been an unhappy arrangement. Josie is one of the most popular girls in our grade. She's best friends with Queen Bee, Sophie Parker, and they're always hanging out with the popular boys like Brendan Dakers and James Tyndale. Josie spends her weekends partying and comes to school wearing a full face of makeup and her hair sprayed perfectly into place.

I spend my weekends reading comics, watching *CSI* with my dad, and complaining about my life to my yellow Labrador, called Dog, who is the only creature on this planet who listens to me. And I can only get him to listen if I'm holding a bit of bacon.

So I skipped out the part of the story where Josie looked miserably at Brendan, who she was clearly hoping to be partnered with, and then came to sit next to me with a big sigh and no greeting. She didn't even look at me when I went, "Howdy, partner," in a courageous attempt to lighten the atmosphere.

I really don't know why that was the greeting I went with.

She couldn't be bothered to do the experiment, so I just got on with it. Now, technically, Mrs. Ginnwell had not explained the Bunsen burner part of the experiment yet as everyone was putting on their lab coats and goggles. But some people were taking their time, and Josie, leaning on her hand, kept glancing at Brendan, laughing at whatever he was saying to her and flicking her hair dramatically.

I guess this is where it kind of becomes my fault. I should have waited until we were told to start up the Bunsen burners, but I went ahead and turned ours on.

There are a few very important things to remember here:

1. I did not realize it was on the highest flame setting.
2. I did not realize that, just as I turned it on, Josie would flick her hairspray-laden locks in the direction that she did.
3. I did not realize that her hair was quite so flammable.
4. I did not realize that she would run around screaming rather than stay still so that throwing water at her became increasingly difficult, and my aim isn't that good anyway so I actually ended up just soaking myself.
5. I did not expect Mrs. Ginnwell to use so much foam that Josie resembled a poodle.

6. It should also be remembered that I have never been in any real trouble at school before this incident.

7. Apart from that time when I was six and Ben Metton ate my Doritos, so I locked him in the supply closet.

8. The whole fire incident is in fact very upsetting for me too as I didn't mean to do it, I feel awful, and now no one will want to stay friends with me, just like at my last school.

At this point I started crying.

Ms. Duke, who had been staring at me in shock, passed me a tissue. "Well, it sounds to me like it was an accident—" she began.

"Of course it was an accident!" I wailed, interrupting her. "I would never do that on purpose!"

There was a knock on the door, and I turned in my seat to see the school nurse slowly pop her head in. Ms. Duke beckoned her in, and she came forward happily. "I wanted to let you know, Ms. Duke, and you, Anna, that Josie is perfectly fine. Her hair is singed at the end and she'll have to have a haircut, but apart from that she is right as rain."

"She must hate me," I said glumly, staring at the damp, crumpled tissue in my hand.

"I'm sure she doesn't. She'll get over it," the nurse said jovially. "Her hair was so long and straggly anyway, a cut will probably improve things."

"Um, *thank* you, Tricia," Ms. Duke said pointedly. The nurse gave a cheerful shrug and left.

"There you go, that's something," Ms. Duke announced. "It was clearly an accident but one that could have had nasty consequences. We've been lucky, Anna."

I nodded gravely.

"I hope that from now on you won't begin any kind of experiment without instruction."

"I'm never going to do another experiment again."

"I hope you will. Chemistry is a fascinating subject, and I imagine you've learned an important lesson with regards to safety." She looked at me sternly. "Right, well, while we've established this wasn't intentional, I'm going to have to give you detention lasting the remainder of this semester so that you can reflect on the importance of caution. It starts tomorrow. And since it is the end of the day in about ten minutes, you can return to your classroom, gather your things, and go home."

"I'd rather not go back, to be honest."

"You don't need anything?"

"It's just my pencil case and books. People have probably thrown them in the trash by now."

"I'm sure that's not true." Ms. Duke gave a thin smile. "They all know it was an accident and no harm done. By tomorrow they'll have forgotten the whole thing."

It's worrying how clueless adults are sometimes.

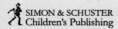